MEET ME IN CENTRAL PARK

JO BARTLETT

Boldwood

First published in 2017. This edition published in Great Britain in 2023 by Boldwood Books Ltd.

Copyright © Jo Bartlett, 2023

Cover Design by Head Design Ltd.

Cover Illustration: Shutterstock and iStock

Every effort has been made to obtain the necessary permissions with reference to copyright material, both illustrative and quoted. We apologise for any omissions in this respect and will be pleased to make the appropriate acknowledgements in any future edition.

A CIP catalogue record for this book is available from the British Library.

Paperback ISBN 978-1-80483-931-7

Large Print ISBN 978-1-80483-930-0

Hardback ISBN 978-1-80483-932-4

Ebook ISBN 978-1-80483-929-4

Kindle ISBN 978-1-80483-928-7

Audio CD ISBN 978-1-80483-937-9

MP3 CD ISBN 978-1-80483-936-2

Digital audio download ISBN 978-1-80483-933-1

Boldwood Books Ltd
23 Bowerdean Street
London SW6 3TN
www.boldwoodbooks.com

This book is all about the way in which friendship can make any place feel like home. As such, it's dedicated to the friends, old and new, who I met on the weekend when the idea for this story (and most of the characters' names) came about, as well as to the people who make my online community feel like home too. I've added a thank you to you all by name in the acknowledgments and I want you to know how much I value your friendship and support xx

1

'Sit down, Libby, I've got something to tell you.' Nan was already pouring brandy into two glasses, which couldn't be a good sign. I'd been about to say we shouldn't be drinking while we were working, but looking around the pub, there weren't any customers to worry about. Our takings for the day would barely have covered the cost of a pickled gherkin each, let alone the huge brandies she was pouring. Maybe the pub takings were what she wanted to talk about? My stomach dropped at the thought. My grandparents couldn't shut the place, though. I'd have nowhere left to go.

'Can you just tell me what it is, please?' Why couldn't she just come out with it? All the preamble did was prolong the agony, and I'd been there before. The fact that Nan felt the need to pour such strong drinks *was* worrying, but I'd already had the worst news in the world. So, whatever it was, it couldn't be that bad.

'We're closing the pub.' Nan shoved one of the glasses towards me.

Finally doing as I was told, and plonking myself down onto a rickety barstool, I picked up the glass and took a big swig. It was like inhaling a tube of Deep Heat. No wonder they gave people brandy for shock – the pain in my oesophagus made it impossible to think about anything else. 'I can't believe you're actually selling up. When did you make that decision?'

'Oh no, we're not *closing* it, closing it.' Nan laughed, and I wondered if she'd started on the brandy before me. She wasn't making any sense and I wasn't finding any of this funny. 'We're just closing up for Christmas.'

She'd said it, the C word. The word we'd made a pact not to mention until the first of December every year – longer, if we could avoid it. But it was only September, and I'd barely got over the Christmas before. I know everyone complains about Christmas decorations appearing in the supermarket aisles in September, but I actually had to hold my breath and run past the seasonal aisle in Sainsbury's. The world seemed to be obsessed with Christmas the moment the school summer holidays were over and, try as I did to hide away from all that – in the world's least-successful micro-pub – it always proved impossible in the end.

It would have been easier to move to a country where they didn't celebrate Christmas at all, but then I'd never exactly been skilled at learning new languages. Five years of schoolgirl French had left me able to repeat '*je ne comprends pas*' in a fairly convincing accent. But it was hardly a basis for believing I'd be fluent in Japanese, given enough time.

I could cope with Christmas Day, because it meant a long shift in the pub – when for once there were more customers than staff – and all I had to do was exchange polite good wishes. There was no way I could sit down to a proper Christmas dinner, though. Not when there were two empty spaces at the table. I never thought I'd miss Mum's dried-out turkey dinners, but I missed *everything* about them. Even Dad's jokes. The last time we'd had Christmas dinner, he'd joked that Noah should've used Mum's recipe to cook the turkeys on the ark, because it would have soaked up the flood in ten minutes flat. She'd laughed, like she always did, and Dad had asked for second helpings of turkey, just as he always did, too.

'I don't understand. Why are you closing for Christmas? It's the only time we ever make a profit.' They couldn't do this to me. No one else but them understood why I could never face a real Christmas again.

'Your granddad's been promising for years that he'll take me to see the Northern Lights. And now that he's had his cataracts done, he's finally got a chance of telling the difference between them and the smears on the car windscreen, which he tried to convince me were a rare glimpse of the lights when we were up in Scotland doing that whisky tasting.'

'And you'll be away for Christmas?' Call me a cynic, but I wasn't convinced Granddad even knew about the trip. He loved the micro-pub he'd set up when he retired, which was barely bigger than a good-sized front room. It had always been more of a hobby to them than a business, though. Most of the customers were friends of my grandparents, and had their own tankards over the bar, only paying cost price for their drinks. It was usually almost impossible to get Granddad to leave the place, unless he was on a road trip with Nan, testing out a new line for the pub, like the Scottish honey whisky he'd brought back the last time. So the idea that he'd willingly suggested going away for Christmas didn't ring true.

'Yes, we're going on a cruise!' Nan whipped a brochure out of her handbag, which more or less had its own seat at the bar. 'We'll be away from the nineteenth to the twenty-ninth; doesn't it look great?'

'Hmm.' Even though I wanted to grab hold of her by the ankles and beg her not to go, I had to think about what was best for them. Nan had always wanted to do this, and Christmas was hard for them too. After all, they'd lost their daughter – their only child – almost two years before. Now they were stuck with me: a fun sponge, if ever there was one. 'I'm sure you'll have a great time, but there's no need to shut the pub. I can manage. It's not like we're ever really rushed off our feet, even at Christmas, and I'm sure Billy would help out if I needed him to.' Billy was at least twice my age, with gout that made it difficult for him to walk, but it didn't seem to affect his ability to stand up and look down my top when he got the chance. Every so often, he'd ask me out on a date, too, and I'd wonder how my life had come to this.

I'd had a boyfriend when my parents died and we'd been talking about moving in together, but after the accident he told me I'd changed. He didn't seem to have any idea why losing both my parents so tragically made such a difference to how I felt about life. At first, he'd tried relentless cheerfulness and, when that hadn't worked, he told me he couldn't waste some of the best years of his life waiting for me to realise that life was too short to spend mourning. I'd expected Ryan ending our relationship to hurt, but I'd felt nothing. Not even anger. Since then, despite Nan's attempts to set me up with almost every unattached male she knew under the age of fifty, I'd had absolutely no desire to even think about another relationship. So, it would be wrong to string Billy along and let him think he might stand a chance – just to convince him to help me out at the pub – but anything was better than not working on Christmas Day.

'Oh no, we're definitely shutting the pub,' Nan said firmly. 'We've told all the regulars already and we're going to have a big party on New Year's Eve to make up for it, with all the drinks on the house.'

'You'll be bankrupt by the second of January at the rate you're going.' I took another sip of brandy. God knows where Granddad had got it from, but it was burning the back of my throat. If I'd been describing it at a tasting, I've had said it had notes of battery acid that had been drained through an old sock.

'It's only money and closing for Christmas is more important. You can't go on like this, Libby; it's been almost two years and that's long enough. Your mum and dad wouldn't have wanted this for you.'

'What do you mean, I can't go on like this?'

'Your counsellor said you've got to face your fears head-on. That means you've got to stop pretending that Christmas doesn't exist. Otherwise this might be it for you: serving Granddad's cronies and cooking just enough steak and ale pies to pay your way, but not making enough money to actually have a life. I can't let it happen, Lib. Not on my watch.'

'I wish I'd never told you what the counsellor said.' I couldn't quite keep my voice from sounding whiney. She was right, though; my counsellor was convinced I'd never get on with my life until I'd learned to celebrate Christmas again. But what no one seemed to understand – not even my lovely grandparents – was that I didn't *want* to get on with my life. I didn't deserve to. My parents were gone and I hadn't done enough to make sure that the person responsible had been punished for it. I didn't deserve to celebrate anything, least of all Christmas.

'Well, you did,' Nan said sternly. 'And one way or another, you're going to have to face up to Christmas this year.'

'What do you suggest I do? Cook myself a turkey dinner and invite Billy round to pull a cracker with me?' I shuddered at the thought. That was actually one of Billy's chat-up lines. Except, in his scenario, I was the cracker.

'No, I've already sorted Christmas for you, too.' Nan's eyelid was twitching, but then she had every right to look nervous.

'What have you done?'

'I've had a phone call from Dottie. She's had to have her hip done, and you know it's her busiest time of year...'

A coldness crept up my spine. 'Oh no. Please tell me you haven't?' My great aunt had a Christmas shop, on Seventh Avenue in New York. But not even Nan could think that was a good idea.

Nan looked resolute. 'She needs someone to help her and you need to be fully immersed in Christmas, according to your counsellor. It's like a match made in heaven.'

'Hell, more like.' I shook my head. 'Look, I'm sorry, Nan, it's a shame about Auntie Dottie, but there's no way I'm going to New York of all places. If it makes you happy, I'll book to have Christmas dinner at the Abode hotel in town, but I can't face Christmas *and* New York. It's just too much.'

'I've already promised Auntie Dottie.'

'Well, you'll just have to un-promise her then.'

'She's desperate. She wouldn't have reached out to me otherwise and she never asks anyone for help. I'd go myself if I could, but I'm not as fit as I used to be and the doctor said at my last check-up that I need a break.' Nan rubbed her back, her face taking on a pained expression.

'Emotional blackmail isn't going to work either.' I was trying to convince myself as much as her, but she knew exactly how to get under my skin. I had to stand firm this time, though.

'I've already booked your flight, for the end of October.'

'You've done *what*?'

'There was a great offer on the flight and I didn't want to miss it. Dottie needs you, but you need this even more.' The twitch in her eyelid was working overtime now, but there were tears welling up too. Much as I wanted to run out into the streets of Canterbury and never look back, I couldn't do it and I couldn't even blame her for what she'd done either. She wanted the old Libby back, the version of me she'd lost on the same day she'd lost her only daughter. But the old Libby was gone, and a trip to New York wasn't going to change that. In fact, it would only make things worse. I needed to think of a way of getting out of this and making Nan see that going to New York was a crazy idea, but flying off the handle and storming out wasn't it.

'I'll think about it.' That was as much as I was prepared to commit to, but judging by the way the expression on Nan's face changed, anyone would think I'd already packed my case.

'It's going to be the start of something wonderful, Lib, just you wait and see.' Nan wrapped her arms around me. 'Last year was so awful for all of us, and watching you go through every first without your mum and dad has killed me inside a little bit each time. I vowed last Christmas that, by the time we got to the second anniversary of life without them, I'd have found a way to finally help you start to move on. I'm just so glad you've agreed to go.'

It was on the tip of my tongue to remind her that I'd hadn't agreed to anything yet, but for now Nan was happy and I didn't want to be the one to take that away from her. There'd be some reason I could come up with later for not being able to go, a problem with my visa ought to do it, and I'd make sure I reimbursed her for the flights. Maybe spending Christmas alone would be a good thing. I wouldn't have to pretend to enjoy a single second of it for anyone else's sake. There was no point in celebrating when the only thing I wanted in the world was something not even Santa could pull off. No one could.

* * *

It had been two weeks since Nan had told me about her plans to ship me off to New York for two months and I still hadn't found a way of telling her that there was no way on earth I was going anywhere. If I'd been prepared to leave my home city for any reason, it would have been to get away *after* Christmas. That was when the worst of the memories hit me. The anniversary of my parents' accident and the updates from the police about the prosecution of the man who'd killed them, were mingled in with the utter bleakness that January always seemed to bring. Then there was Mum's birthday and the promise I'd made her, when I could no longer give her a present, that I'd make sure Grant Bailey paid for what he'd done. But I'd failed at that too. I'd sat in a court room months later, staring into his face, looking for a shred of recognition of what he'd done to our family, but there was none.

The court had asked us to prepare a victim impact statement. When I sat down with my grandparents to put it together, it was as if someone had peeled back the top layer of their skin and all the raw anguish that they'd been pushing down to protect me was laid bare. It was almost as devastating as the accident itself had been, but not quite. It was me who wrote up the final statement, trying to pull together the things we'd spoken about in a way that captured the impact of my parents' death. But there was no way to do that justice and I couldn't convey the anguish on my grandparents' faces in words alone. I could still repeat one of the sections I wrote word for word, though, as if it was permanently burned into my brain.

Life without them will never be the same. It will never be as whole, or a as good, or as happy as it used to be when they were here. We'll never be truly happy again now they're gone.

My grandmother had sobbed when she'd read it and at first, I'd thought it was because of all the feelings those words represented, but she'd told me it wasn't that. It was the idea that I believed I could never be truly happy again that broke her heart.

'I wouldn't have been able to go on if it wasn't for you, Lib.' Nan had taken my face in her hands. 'Losing your mum has been the hardest thing I've ever been through, but I can see so much of her in you. When she had you, she got to fulfil her biggest dream and become a mum. That's why we've got to choose to be happy for all the things she did get to do and, as much as we'll always wish she was still here, she wouldn't want any of us to spend the rest of our lives being unhappy because she's gone. So you can't write that Lib, because I can't bear the thought that it might be true.'

I hadn't wanted to argue with her, not when the pain was imprinted so clearly in her expression. But I'd meant every word. At the time, I couldn't believe I'd ever remember how to laugh again. And what was more, I didn't think I wanted to remember. Yet for Nan's sake, I took that part out of the statement and I'll never know if that's why the judge made the decision he did.

Four years. That's what Grant Bailey got for killing both of my parents. The judge was able to sentence him for death by driving whilst disqualified, because of a previous conviction for driving under the influence of drugs and alcohol. But delays in testing Bailey at the hospital, where he quickly recovered from the minor injuries he'd sustained during the crash, meant the results were inconclusive. There were traces of both alcohol and drugs in his system, but it wasn't enough to convict him of death by dangerous driving.

Hearing the judge read out his sentence and seeing the relief flood Grant Bailey's face was the second worst day of my life and, as far as I was concerned, he'd got away with murder. After that, I became obsessed with getting his sentence reviewed. I wrote to my MP, the Attorney General, every newspaper I could think of, but all of it had come to nothing. My parents had probably been robbed of thirty years and all Grant Bailey was going to miss out on was four years of his life, or at least I'd thought so.

'Have you heard back about your visa yet?' It was the third time in the last forty-eight hours that Nan had asked me the question, but there was something different about this time. Every other time she'd mentioned it, she'd rolled her eyes and gently chided me for not getting it sorted out, but now there was a strained look on her face and she was moving from foot to foot, as if the floor was suddenly too hot to stand on.

'Not yet, but I'll chase them again tomorrow.' I was beginning to sound like a stuck record and I expected Nan to sigh, but when her face crumpled, I knew I was right about something being different this time around.

'Nan, what's wrong?' When I put my arm around her shoulders, she was shaking. This wasn't about my trip to New York and, as soon as I looked into her eyes, I had a terrible feeling I knew what was coming.

'I've had a phone call saying they're preparing to release Grant Bailey on probation.' Nan's voice cracked, and it was all I could do not to scream, even though the desire to do so was burning in my throat. The man who'd been seen drinking and smoking cannabis, in the hours before getting into his car and driving my parents off the road, was getting out of prison.

'How can this be happening? He hasn't even served half of his sentence yet.' I squeezed my eyes shut, because if I started to cry, I might not be able to stop and I needed to know exactly what my grandmother had been told.

'It's coming up to the halfway point, and they're moving him to an open prison, where he'll be able to have visits home. Then they're going to release him on licence. There are too many criminals and not enough prison spaces apparently.' Nan shook her head. 'Bailey will probably be home with his family on a home visit over Christmas.'

'They can't do this.' Nausea swirled in my stomach and there was a very good chance I was going to be sick. But there was an even stronger feeling pulsing in my veins: white hot rage. I'd never considered myself to be someone capable of violence. Not until my path had crossed with Grant Bailey's.

'I don't know, but they have and there's nothing we can do about it.' Nan suddenly grabbed hold of my wrist. 'I want you to promise me you're not going to try to do anything about it, Lib. Please.'

The pleading look in her eyes twisted something in my gut. She was terrified of losing me too, I knew that, and I shook my head slowly. All the letters and phone calls, and rage and sorrow of the past two years had done nothing to change any of it. Now Grant Bailey would probably be spending time with his family this Christmas, whilst my parents were side by side in the ground. I desperately wanted to believe this couldn't be true, even though I knew it was.

Grant Bailey's parents only lived about ten minutes away from my grandparents' pub. There was every chance one of us could bump into him, and I was worried that I might really be capable of killing him, if I saw him out enjoying himself. It would be easy just to put my foot on the accelerator and deliver the ultimate form of karma. Because, if this was justice, then the law really was an ass. Before the accident, coming home to Canterbury had always felt like my safe place. If I went out for a drink in the evening, I'd never once felt scared walking home. Back when I was at school, my friends and I would walk out of town, following the path of the river, towards the villages on the outskirts and spend all day by the water if we felt like it. It was quaint and quirky and most of all it was home, but Bailey had even managed to take that feeling away from me, because nowhere felt safe after the accident.

'How the hell is this fair? He's going to get to spend Christmas with whoever he wants to this year and we're never going to be able to do that again.' It was like someone was sitting on my chest and suffocating me. I wanted to get out, run away, but it was impossible when the place you wanted to escape from was your own body, your own mind.

'I know, love. I'm so sorry.' Nan sniffed, and I put my arms around her again, breathing in the familiar scent of her lily of the valley perfume, which always smelt like home.

'Oh God! I don't know if I'm going to be able to deal with it. What if I see him when I'm in my car? I honestly don't know what I'd be capable of, but I can picture myself doing the same thing to him as he did to Mum and Dad.'

'You couldn't do it, Lib. Not when it came down to it. But I hate him, too – for what he did to your mum and dad, and what that's done to you.'

'I'm all right, Nan.' I had to be, for her and Granddad; it's what I'd told myself over and over again in the weeks and months that had followed the accident, but she knew me far too well for that.

'Of course you're not all right, not after that news. But you're only human and I wouldn't expect you to be. Just try to remember that it wouldn't matter if they kept that scumbag Bailey in prison for the rest of his life – it wouldn't bring them back. But we want *you* back and it's what your mum and dad would have wanted, much more than seeing Bailey rot in a cell. This makes it feel even more like Dottie's offer has come at just the right time. You know we love you more than anything, Lib, but we all need a break from the memories if we're going to heal. Every time you drive by the road where it happened and pass your old school, where your mum used to pick you up every day, or your dad's favourite restaurant, it hits you all over again, doesn't it?'

'How did you know?' I could visualise my parents in all of those places and suddenly, before she even answered, I knew my grandmother could too.

'Because it's the same for me and your granddad. Why do you think we spend all our time in this dingy old pub? But we've got to break those habits, Lib. Maybe it'll be the cruise for me, or maybe it'll be something else. But I just feel in my water that it's going to be New York for you. You need to get away from here for a little while. Be somewhere without so many reminders of the past.'

'Okay.' It was just a single word, and it was out of my mouth before I even had the chance for second thoughts. I wouldn't stay there for Christmas, though, whatever my grandmother said. There was no way I could stay in a place where the magic of the holidays was evident on every street corner, not when the people I'd loved most in the world had been robbed of their chance to ever celebrate Christmas again, or to even visit the place they'd always dreamed of going. But there'd be no pretence about denied visas and no more trying to talk my grandparents out of what they thought was best for me. I was going to New York, whether I liked it or not. And with Grant Bailey's release on home visits imminent, my flight couldn't leave a moment too soon.

2

———————

'You should have seen this place last night! It was like every crazy in the state of New York wanted to get into *my* cab.'

I tried to keep up with the taxi driver's rapid delivery, as I caught my first glimpse of the Manhattan skyline. But my stomach was churning, and not just because he seemed determined to cut up every other driver using the Grand Central Parkway on the journey from JFK. I'd been so excited on my first trip to New York, five years earlier, but everything had been so different then. And, if I'd never had that trip, I might never have bought my parents the plane tickets for Mum's fiftieth birthday...

'I guess it's like that, working on Halloween.' I mumbled my response, although I wasn't sure the cab driver even heard me. He seemed to be using the trip as an opportunity to offload and kept up his chat all the way to Manhattan, but I didn't take in much else of what he said; I was too busy concentrating on just breathing in and out. I was going to be on Seventh Avenue in a matter of minutes, and the stomach churning was getting worse.

When he pulled up outside my great aunt's Christmas shop, I

could see the neon lights in Times Square, up ahead. 'This is it then, Candy Cane Lane on Seventh.'

I paid the driver and watched the cab join a queue of traffic, as I stood on the sidewalk with my suitcases. Sooner or later, I was going to have to go in, but I couldn't seem to persuade my feet to move.

'Liberty, is that you!' Aunt Dottie's unmistakeable voice carried down the street before I even saw her. But, moments later, she was parting the crowds as her metallic purple mobility scooter came into view. I wasn't sure if she'd dyed her hair to match the scooter – or bought the scooter to match her hair – but either way, it was a striking combination.

'Auntie Dottie.' I bent down to kiss her as she brought her scooter to a halt, narrowly missing my feet. 'You look even younger than the last time I saw you.'

'Well, you know what they say, Libby, you're only as old as the man you feel!' Dottie threw back her head and laughed. 'And luckily for me, the current one is only sixty-one!'

I shook my head but couldn't help but smile. She'd managed to make me laugh within the first two minutes – maybe it was going to be okay, after all. Aunt Dottie's personality was so big it could easily overshadow Christmas, and my counsellor was probably right; I could do with a bit of fun in my life. Hearing about Dottie's antics would certainly be entertaining. At seventy-six, she was two years older than Nan, and still nowhere near ready to settle down.

'His name's Brian and he's been an absolute rock since my hip replacement. He's got elevator service in his building too, so I've been staying there since the operation. Which means you'll have the apartment above the shop all to yourself.' Dottie laughed again. 'And a girl's gotta have the space to entertain, if you know what I mean!'

'Oh, don't worry, I'm not planning on doing anything other

than working while I'm here and helping you out as much as I possibly can. The sort of complications men tend to bring are the last thing I need.'

'Not you, honey, *me*!' Dottie had lived in the States for over thirty years, following a messy divorce, and her English accent had all but disappeared. 'Although, according to Ruby, it is about time *you* saw some action too.'

'Auntie Dottie, please!' It was bad enough that Nan and my great aunt were discussing my love life, but the fact that I was lagging behind a septuagenarian was a new low, even for me.

'Okay, I promise not to nag you about all of that too much. But you never know, New York's a romantic place. Carriage rides in Central Park, sailing around Liberty Island at sunset. Trust me, I've done them all.'

'Like I said, I'm just here to help you out.'

'About that.' Dottie prodded the handlebar of her mobility scooter. 'I'm kinda reliant on this thing right now, so I'm only popping into the shop every now and again. Don't worry, though, you've got help. My friend Betty does as many days as she can fit in around her grandkids, and Madison's full time now.'

'I'm sure we'll manage.' I took a deep breath. This was going to be hard, but working in a shop like Candy Cane Lane there was no way to keep avoiding it; it was time to confront Christmas head-on. 'So, are we going in?'

'Just let me back this thing up; there's a bit of a step-up into the shop. It's perfectly accessible for wheelchairs and strollers, but I need a bit of a run-up to get over it.' True to her word, Dottie reversed the scooter to the furthest edge of the sidewalk, as I pulled open the door. It was certainly one way to make an entrance, and, somehow, she managed not to knock a single ornament off the display in the centre of the shop.

'Morning girls! This is my great niece, Liberty. As you know, she'll be taking over as manager until I get back.' Dottie stopped her scooter by a big artificial Christmas tree dominating the floor space in the shop, which had loads of different baubles hanging on it. They were clearly aimed at appealing to the tourists, as there were miniature Empire State Buildings, Statues of Liberty and yellow taxi cabs decorated with Christmas wreaths. I concentrated on my breathing again. I could cope with Christmas, I was almost sure of it. I just had to stop myself hyperventilating at the thought of spending nearly two months in New York's answer to Santa's grotto.

A young woman, who couldn't have been much older than eighteen or nineteen, flashed me a smile. She had the whitest teeth I'd ever seen in real life. 'Good to meet you, Liberty. I'm Madison. Welcome to New York!'

I returned her smile. 'Nice to meet you too, Madison. But call me Libby, please, almost everyone does.'

'I think Liberty's a lovely name.' The older lady standing next to Madison walked around from the other side of the counter. It didn't take a rocket scientist to work out that she must be Betty. 'And Dottie tells me you were named after Lady Liberty herself?'

'I don't usually tell people that!' I forced a smile; it was true. Back when I was younger, I'd kept it quiet because I'd been embarrassed about being named after a massive green statue. But lately, it was because it reminded me so much of Mum, and the fact that she'd never got to see the statue, or the city she'd loved from afar for so long, for herself.

'Libby it is then, sugar. I'm Betty.' Hugging me as if I was *her* long-lost great niece, she reminded me so much of Nan that a pang of homesickness for my grandparents unexpectedly hit me. I'd been so worried about being in New York for two months, and working in a Christmas shop of all places, that I hadn't even thought about missing them. But before I could dwell on the feeling, Dottie clapped her hands together.

'Now that the introductions are out of the way, I think the best way for you to get to know the shop is to unpack the stock that arrived this morning.' Aunt Dottie made it sound like an order, rather than a suggestion, but anything that kept me busy was fine by me. I thought she might have given me a day or two to get over the flight, before she put me to work, but I'd forgotten that my great aunt had boundless energy, and expected everyone else to be the same. 'You can put your bags up in the apartment and then Madison will show you what's what. I need to borrow Betty for a long-overdue lunch, but I'm sure you two youngsters can cope without us.'

'Of course we can.' Madison was already passing Betty her handbag. 'We'll be fine by ourselves, won't we, Libby?'

'Absolutely.' Giving Dottie a kiss goodbye, and leaving Madison to watch the shop, I took my cases up the narrow staircase to the rooms above. Calling it an apartment was probably stretching it a bit – it certainly didn't look like any of the New York apartments I'd seen in the movies. The boiler was making a growling noise as I put my cases in the small bedroom that was just about big enough for a double bed. At least I hoped it was the boiler. The bathroom was even smaller than the bedroom – but it would do the job – and the living room had windows that looked down on to Seventh Avenue. Mum would have loved it. Just being amongst the buzz of the city, which had been at the top of her wish list to visit, would have been more than enough for her. So who was I to complain?

For just a split second, when I turned back towards the bedroom, I thought I saw a female figure in the corner of the room. 'Oh God.' I breathed the words out in a rush of relief when I realised it was just a dressing gown, hanging on a hook. But for the briefest of moments, it had felt like Mum had been right there with me. If this was what jet lag could do to you, then Dottie's decision to put me straight to work might turn out to be a big mistake. With my head all over the place like this, I could end up giving customers more in change than they'd paid in the first place.

I shook myself, and my stomach rumbled as the smell of pizza wafted in from the Italian restaurant across the street. There was a kitchen area in one corner of the living room, but with the gorgeous aromas drifting in from the deli next door too, I wasn't anticipating doing a lot of cooking during my time here. My only worry was whether my hips would still be able to make it down the narrow staircase by the time I left New York. But that was a problem for another day; for now, my priority was to get to grips with managing Candy Cane Lane.

Madison turned out to be a good teacher. By the middle of the afternoon, she'd shown me how to use the till, explained the ordering system, and helped me unpack a shipment of wooden gingerbread men, which could be personalised with stencils. I wasn't sure I was quite up to that yet, but luckily Madison enjoyed that part of the job best. So I was hoping I'd be able to leave most of that to her, on the days she was in the shop.

The real reason she'd been so keen for Dottie and Betty to go off to lunch soon became clear – she wanted to ask my advice about her boyfriend – and from the moment she started to speak, I knew I was going to be almost useless in giving her the guidance she was looking for.

'He's made some mistakes, sure. But I think all guys my age are gonna do that, right?' Madison didn't even wait for my answer. 'I tried to talk to Betty about it earlier, but she's kinda old school, you know? I thought with you being a bit younger you might think differently about whether cheating's just cheating, or if there are different levels to it?'

I was tempted to tell her that what I knew about men could have been written on the back of one of the little gingerbread men's buttons. But I wasn't planning to start a conversation that might lead to me revealing more than I wanted to. Just because I hadn't had a boyfriend in over two years, it didn't mean I couldn't offer advice. And the truth was I was still reeling from Madison's comment about me being 'a bit younger' than Betty.

'I've got to say that cheating, in any form, has always been a deal breaker for me... What exactly did he do?'

Madison sighed. 'Drank too much and woke up in some girl's dorm room, but he says he can't remember doing anything. So I don't even know if he did really cheat.'

I suddenly felt every bit as old as Madison clearly had me pegged for, and I wanted to take hold of her by the shoulders and tell her she could do so much better. 'Does it really matter if he did or not? He either had the intention to go back there with her, or he got so drunk he can't account for his actions. Neither of those things paint him in a very good light.'

'He did say he's sorry and he's never been in a situation like this before.' Madison looked all wide-eyed and hopeful, which somehow made my response come out all the sharper.

'Oh, well that's okay then.'

'So you think he's for real?' She clearly hadn't picked up on my sarcasm. 'I just can't decide whether I believe him enough to give him another chance, or if I should do what my sister says and bail while I can.' Madison frowned as if this really was a dilemma that needed careful consideration, and I tried to imagine what it was like to be her age and in love. The trouble was, I wasn't sure if I'd ever actually been in love, and certainly not when I was that young. Aunt Dottie was probably the one Madison should have turned to for advice – we'd already established she was far more successful with the opposite sex than me – but I ploughed on anyway.

'If it was me,' I said gently, 'I wouldn't give him a second chance to do anything like that again.' I really wanted to shout, 'dump him and run', but I held my tongue.

'That's what Cherise said. But I really don't want to be on my own for the holidays.' Madison pulled a face, and I was about to tell her that, at her age, worrying about being single should be the last thing on her mind, but then the door to the shop swung open.

'It's true then? There's another Brit on the block!' It seemed Madison wasn't the only one in Manhattan with a Hollywood smile. The two men who'd come into the shop grinned at me, seeming to know exactly who I was, and I wondered how much Aunt Dottie had said. The last thing I wanted was sympathy or knowing looks.

'Libby, this is Dannie and Rob; they run the deli next door.' Madison turned to me. 'And you'll never guess what, Dannie's from England too! So I'm sure the two of you will have lots to talk about.'

'Welcome to the Big Apple, chicken.' Dannie had a distinctive Yorkshire accent with just the edge knocked off. 'This is my partner, Rob, but he prefers to be referred to as *the hot older guy*.' Dannie laughed, and Rob shook his head.

'You make a joke after a few too many beers and Dannie never lets you forget it.' Rob smiled. 'He's been so excited that he'll have someone to talk about the weather with, since Dottie told him you were coming over. That's what passes as entertainment for you guys, isn't it?'

'He doesn't really believe in all those stereotypes, you know! He's just trying to get his own back. Although, I've got to admit, New York provides plenty of scope for talking about the weather. Sometimes we get all four seasons in one day.' Dannie picked up a

Swarovski crystal bauble, putting it back when Rob shook his head.

'See what I mean? He can't help himself. He's a typical Brit; he even pays a small fortune to have Yorkshire teabags flown in. He went cold turkey once when the delivery didn't show up. Never again!' Rob pretended to shudder, and I had to laugh. I was with Dannie on that; I couldn't function without a good cup of tea in the mornings. But I wasn't about to confess. Madison would be shipping us off to lunch with Betty and Dottie at this rate. Although I had a feeling my great aunt was more of a Long Island Iced Tea sort of girl.

'It's good to meet you both. I was planning to come into the deli later anyway to stock up. I'm not much of a cook, so you might be seeing a lot of me.' I took after Mum in that respect. I couldn't even cook plain pasta without burning half of it onto the bottom of the pan. I'd inherited her colouring too – fair with blonde hair, and blue eyes. But I had dad's dry sense of humour – at least I had done, when there'd still been things to laugh about.

Dannie's eyes lit up. 'We'll cook for you, next week. How about that?' Dannie looked at Rob and laughed again. 'Okay, to be fair, Rob will cook for you, and I'll pour the drinks. That's much more my forte, isn't it darling?'

'Sure is, but it's a great idea anyway. How about you, Madison, are you free for dinner next week?'

'I'm supposed to be doing stuff with Scott next week, so I'll let you know.' Madison had been furiously texting the whole time Dannie and Rob had been talking. I hoped she'd see sense about her cheating boyfriend. But I had a feeling it might take her a while.

'Let us know then, Mads.' Dannie didn't look the slightest bit offended that dinner with him and Rob was only her backup plan.

'Shall we say Thursday then, Libby? I might even dig out a Yorkshire teabag for you, if you play your cards right!'

'Sounds good.' I watched them leave, slightly bemused by their whirlwind of a visit, but feeling a little lighter somehow. Maybe Nan had been right about me needing a Christmas away from home. In New York I could be anyone. I didn't have to be the tragic girl who'd lost both her parents in a car crash. And maybe I could even forget, just for a few weeks, that the man who was responsible for all of that would soon be going home.

3

In the end, I decided to get my first night's dinner from Ray's Famous Pizza, a couple of blocks up from Candy Cane Lane. Aunt Dottie had invited me for dinner with her and Brian, but I'd taken a rain check. I was tired and in need of comfort food, and nothing hit the spot like pepperoni pizza. She'd also let it slip that they were celebrating their six-month anniversary, and I didn't feel like playing gooseberry to my great aunt and her toy boy. It must have been the right thing to do, because she'd given me the next day off. Betty and Madison were both booked in to work, anyway, and Dottie had suddenly mentioned the possibility of jetlag. I had a feeling I'd been right about her reasons for setting me to work straight away: she'd known I needed the distraction to help me get settled in and try to forget about everything I'd left behind back at home.

Aunt Dottie had been an all-too-infrequent visitor to the UK when I was growing up, but she'd always made a big impression. Mum had been obsessed with New York for as long as I could remember, watching as many movies and TV series set there as she could get her hands on. I think she knew every line in every episode of *Friends* off by heart. And she lit up like a Christmas tree every time Dottie came home for a visit. She'd been planning a trip to New York for as long as I could remember, too. But something always seemed to get in the way – usually money, or the lack of it. Mum had found out she was expecting me when my parents were barely out of their teens, and they'd been playing catch-up ever since.

They'd scrimped and saved throughout my childhood to make sure I'd never miss out on opportunities, even helping to pay my way through university when the time came. And just after I graduated, Dad got made redundant. He found a new job eventually, but they were back to playing catch-up with their debts again by then, and desperately saving to be in a position to start their own business. In the meantime, I'd got a well-paid job in corporate law for a firm that had offices in several countries. It meant I jumped ahead of Mum and got a couple of all-expenses-paid business trips to New York. She was thrilled for me, but I could tell it made her want to visit even more. It was what I wanted for her, too, and my mum's fiftieth birthday seemed like too good an opportunity to miss. I had the money to treat them and, after all they'd done for me, it felt so good to finally be doing something to pay them back, just a tiny bit. It was meant to be the trip of a lifetime, but they never even made it to the airport.

Waking up on my first full day in New York, my parents were on my mind – just as they would have been if I'd woken up in the little single bed in my grandparents' spare room above the micro-pub in Kent. For the first few months after they'd died, I was obsessed with counting the days and weeks since they'd set off on their trip. It got easier to stop doing that after a year of firsts – my first birthday without them there for Mum to bake one of her cakes with the consistency of a rubber ball, the first Mothering

Sunday, and Father's Day. And, worst of all, the first Christmas. But they were never far from my thoughts, whatever day it was.

I was up early despite not setting an alarm, an exhausting day of travelling, and getting to grips with the systems in the shop. But my body didn't seem to want to rest. I peered out of the gap in the open window and on to Seventh Avenue. The sidewalks were already busy, despite how early it was. People in business suits, who looked like nothing could stop them until they reached their destination, jostled for space with others who were carrying bags, looking ready to hit the shops as soon as they opened. Then there were the tourists who thought nothing of blocking the sidewalk altogether, as they stopped to snap pictures of the most famous city in the world on their mobile phones. All human life was here, just as Mum had known it would be. She'd have liked nothing better than people watching and, if she'd been with me, we'd have been playing the game we often played – trying to guess people's jobs and backgrounds, where they came from and what they were doing here. It was like giving everyone we saw a fictional life story and I had kept telling Mum she should write a book.

'One day.' She'd said that far too often, always thinking there was plenty of time left for all of that, but it had run out before any of us had believed possible.

'I hope we get snow while we're here.' I was still talking to Mum as if she was in the room with me. If anyone else had heard, they'd probably have decided that I'd finally lost the plot, but I needed to find a way to cope with being here. I'd decided on the flight, when all I could think about was how excited Mum would have been the moment we took off, that while I was here, I'd pretend she could see everything that I could. I didn't know how long I could keep it up, but for now it was helping.

'It's way too early for anything like that yet, but it feels colder than yesterday already.' It was the first of November and the weather seemed to have realised that another month had been flipped over on the calendar, because there was definitely more of a nip in the air. 'I might even have to borrow Aunt Dottie's dressing gown.'

Pulling the window shut, I turned towards where the dressing gown, which had scared the life out of me the day before, was hanging. Unhooking it, I breathed in, inhaling a scent that made it feel more than ever as if my mother was right by my side. Like Nan, Mum had had a favourite perfume she'd always worn: Youth Dew. It was her one indulgence, even when money was tight. I'd given her a bottle the Christmas before she'd died, and Mum had acted as if it was a lovely, unexpected surprise, the way she always did, despite the fact I'd bought her a bottle for Christmas ever since I could remember. Even before I was earning my own money, Dad used to get one and let me write the label, as if it was from me.

'Look inside the box.' I'd smiled, barely able to contain my excitement, waiting for her to open the gift set to discover the plane tickets and hotel booking I'd made in my parents' names. 'There's a little something extra in there for you.'

It had taken her a moment or two to find the envelope and take in what the contents meant, but then she'd reacted exactly as I'd known she would. 'Oh my God, Libs, really?'

There'd been happy tears and laughter and so much excitement that day, and a bit of panic from Mum about how they could get everything organised to leave in less than three weeks' time. It was one of the reasons why I'd cleared it all with my dad first and made sure he could request leave from work for him and Mum, and sort out things like visas. I'd been so thrilled with how perfectly I'd planned it, making sure that nothing could possibly go wrong, but then Grant Bailey had smashed into their car and my whole world had gone more horribly wrong than I could ever have imagined it going.

'If you're here, Mum, just give me a sign.' The goosepimples and the hairs standing up on my arms had nothing to do with the drop in temperature, because when I pressed the dressing gown against my face, it was like someone had liberally sprayed it with Youth Dew just seconds before.

'Mum? Are you here?' I waited again, but there was nothing. Just an old dressing gown, a lingering scent in the air that Aunt Dottie had probably been wearing the last time she'd had the dressing gown on, and far too much imagination. Just because I wanted Mum to be here with me, it didn't mean she was.

'I think I need some air.' This time I really was talking to myself. I had no idea why, but what I did know was that I had to clear my head and get out and walk. It was a coping mechanism I'd used a lot since the accident, and I must have walked every street in Canterbury a hundred times. But with Central Park just a few blocks away from the shop, I now had a whole new place to escape to.

I'd never got round to visiting Central Park on any of my business trips, but it had been number one on Mum's wish list. If she couldn't do it, I was just going to have to do it for her.

As soon as I stepped onto the first path, I sensed that I'd been there before. I knew I hadn't, of course, but it *felt* so much like I had. The knot between my shoulder blades seemed to undo. Maybe it was the oasis of calm it provided in such a frenetic city, but I fell in love with the park from the start. There were huge office blocks and apartment buildings all around, and it was like being dropped into a piece of woodland amongst all of that. A few dog walkers and joggers were around, but it was unexpectedly quiet, and to my surprise there were even parts of the walk where I felt as if I was completely alone. I'd never have imagined finding such peace and solitude just moments away from the throng of the crowds, but this felt like the corner of New York I was always meant to find.

Most of the trees were still clinging on to their leaves, and the colours were as beautiful as I'd always thought they'd be: rusty orange, earthy browns, deep reds and shades of yellow. Mum would have been picking up leaves from the ground and stuffing them in her bag 'for later'.

'We're not just making memories, we're taking memories, aren't we Libs?' It was what she'd always said when she was filling her bag with pebbles or shells from a visit to the beach, even though she knew she wasn't really supposed to, or taking home ticket stubs from a trip to the movies. She'd had about ten memory boxes and even more scrapbooks, which had all been packed into the loft at my grandparents' place after my parents had died.

'Are you sure you aren't just saying that as an excuse to hoard all kinds of rubbish?' Dad would tease her about collecting so much stuff and she'd always say the same thing about that too.

'Just as well for you that I don't mind holding on to old things for decades, isn't it!' I could see them now, laughing together, before Dad pulled her into his arms and told her just how grateful he was that she'd decided to keep hold of him for all these years. They'd have been having that same old exchange as they strolled through Central Park, I was certain of it. And suddenly it wasn't just Mum I could almost feel walking by my side. It was stupid, but I felt closer to Mum and Dad, standing in that park, than I ever had in their old house after they were gone. I'd wanted so badly to believe the well-meaning words of comfort, after they'd first died – *they'll always be with you* – but I could never *feel* it. Not until I'd arrived in New York. Maybe the jetlag really was getting to me after all, but I didn't care. I wanted to hold on to the sensation of my parents walking alongside me for as long as I possibly could, so I kept going. I went all the way from the south end of the park to the north end, and back again, climbing up to Belvedere Castle to look at the view.

'It feels like I'm on the set of a film.' I hadn't intended to say the words out loud, but I must have done, because someone answered me.

'I'm sorry, were you talking to me?' Looking up, I locked eyes with a tall man giving me a quizzical look and heat flushed from my collarbone, all the way up my neck to my cheeks.

'Oh, no, sorry. I was just thinking out loud.' He was wearing a park ranger's uniform, so he'd probably seen it all: flashers, tourists jumping into the fountains, and plenty of people, like me, talking to themselves. But, for some reason, I didn't want him to think I was weird. Although why on earth it mattered to me what this complete stranger thought, I'll never know. 'I just recognise so much of this place, even though I've never been here before, and I'm sure I've seen this castle in a film?'

'Well, it was Gargamel's headquarters in the Smurf movie.' The man laughed. 'Although it's been in much better movies than that, too.'

'What would you say if I admitted it was the Smurf movie I remembered it from?' I looked at him properly for the first time, and got that same sense of déjà vu I'd had when I came into the park. As though I'd met him before somewhere.

'I wouldn't judge you; everyone's got their eccentricities.' He laughed again, and there was another jolt of recognition. I *must* have met him before, but I had no idea where.

'So, do you work here? In the park, I mean?' I should probably just have made my excuses and left – he already thought I talked to myself, and that my favourite movie was *The Smurfs* – but I had to find out where I knew him from, or it was going to drive me mad.

'I'm an urban ranger.' He pulled a face. 'That makes it sound like something out of a video game, or like I should be wearing a spandex suit with a bolt of lightning on the front and a matching cape, but it's far less exciting in reality. What it really means, is that I help maintain the park's ecosystem and give talks to schoolkids about the nature that's all around them in the city. Especially what they can see here, in the park, if they look up from their phones every once in a while, which, as you can imagine, takes a lot of persuasion.'

'Have you always worked here?' I must have sounded like I was interviewing him for a job or auditioning for the role of his stalker. But it was probably part of his job description to be nice to tourists, whatever inane questions they asked.

'More or less, since I came out of college, anyway. I'm Harry by the way.' He held out his hand, and, when I took it, there was that strange sense of connection again. If I'd believed in all that sort of stuff, I could've convinced myself we'd met in a past life. But there had to be a simple explanation for it – fate had never done much for me in the past. If he hadn't said he'd always worked in the park, I'd have assumed I'd met him on one of my visits to the New York offices in my previous job. But I don't think I'd have forgotten Harry in a hurry and it was bugging the hell out of me.

Maybe it could be explained by synchronicity, the coincidence of bumping into the same stranger, over and over again. I'd probably stood next to him in the queue for the Staten Island Ferry on my last visit, or sat next to him at a Broadway show. After all, he had a face I would have unconsciously committed to memory. If it had been three years earlier, I might even have given him my number, or asked for his. I was bold back then, convinced that life was for the taking and that somewhere out there I'd find my other half, just like Mum and Dad, and Nan and Granddad had found theirs. As it was, those sorts of feelings had died when my parents did. I no longer believed in happy ever afters and, the truth was, I was scared of allowing myself to love anyone else who I might end up losing. I already had to face the fact that my grandparents were getting older. If I started another relationship, the chances of it going all the way to the end were less than fifty/fifty, even if I made it as far as the altar one day. And that was just the chance of the relationship breaking down, it didn't take into account freak accidents, or losing someone to an illness. I couldn't risk it and, if that meant being on my own, I didn't care. At least that way I'd be safe from further hurt. Not even the man standing in front of me, who had possibly the best smile I'd ever seen, could convince me to think otherwise.

'So, I can hear the British accent... What brings you to New York?'

'I've just taken a holiday job, working in my great aunt's Christmas shop, until the end of the year.'

'Not Candy Cane Lane?'

'It is, actually.' I wondered if he was going to give me a lecture about how many Christmas decorations ended up in landfill, or tell me that they took three million years to biodegrade. He'd already mentioned ecosystems, so he probably wasn't the sort of person who'd have a replica Statue of Liberty hanging from his Christmas tree. Maybe I should just have kept my big mouth shut.

'I used to love that shop when I was a kid!' Harry smiled, and I found myself hoping for a bit more synchronicity. Besides, if chance meant I bumped into him, the situation was out of my hands. That was very different to taking active steps to make it happen. 'I've still got a wooden nutcracker toy that my grand-mother had engraved for me there, when I was about eight. And I carried on her tradition of buying one new decoration every

December. I've pointed plenty of tourists in that direction over the years, too. My friends run the deli next door, so I've met your aunt several times. She's quite a character.'

'She is.' It wouldn't have surprised me if everyone on Manhattan Island knew who Dottie was. 'I'm Libby, by the way, if you need any help picking out your new decoration for this year.' It sounded like the worst chat-up line, ever and I inwardly cringed at just how awkward I was being.

'I'll bear that in mind. It's nice to meet you, Libby.' The poor guy must have been desperately thinking of a way to end the conversation. 'I've got a school visit in a little while, but I'm sure I'll see you in the shop at some point.'

'Uh-huh.' If that hadn't been a very polite brush-off then I didn't know what was, but explaining that I hadn't been propositioning him would just have made things even more awkward. With any luck, the synchronicity had run out after all. One thing was certain, I was completely out of the habit of having a normal conversation with men of my own age, and suddenly the idea of gently rebuffing Billy's hopeful advances back at the micro-pub didn't seem so bad.

'I really hope you enjoy your stay in New York, Libby.'

'Thank you.' I turned to look back across the lake below the castle, as Harry walked away. One thing that working in the shop might do, was to remind me how to talk to new people again. Nan had said I'd been hiding myself away for too long, and I was starting to think she might be right.

* * *

I didn't want to leave the park, even though the rumbling in my stomach was more than capable of scaring off the flock of birds perched on the edge of the lake in front of the Loeb Boathouse.

Re-energised after a buying a sandwich that could have fed a small family, I headed back towards the south end of the park, stopping to read some of the plaques on the benches that lined the main paths. Some of them were in memoriam, but there were lots of dedications of love, too. They were all touching, in their own way, but there was one that stopped me, a familiar burning sensation catching in the back of my throat.

To Grace ~ From Charlie

We fell in love in this park and shared our life in this city – through laughter, tears, and a million precious memories. She was mine before we even met, and I was hers. Always.

There was a love story – right there – on a plaque about the size of a postcard. Whoever Charlie was, he'd summed up his feelings for Grace perfectly. I could recognise it, even though I'd never felt that way about someone. Because I'd seen it in Mum and Dad. My only comfort, when I'd lost them, was that they'd gone together. It made the pain doubly hard to bear, for those of us left behind, but I don't think they could have lived without each other. Wiping my eyes furiously, in a fruitless attempt to stem the tears, I turned and walked straight into Harry.

'Libby! Fancy bumping into you again so soon.' His smile slid off his face as he looked at me properly for the first time. 'Hey, what's wrong?'

'I'm fine.' Even as I said the words, I started to sob. I hated anyone seeing me crying, but, once I'd given in to the tears, there was no way I'd be able to stop.

'You don't look fine to me. Come on, let me get you a drink in the Ranger Center. I can find somewhere quiet, and you can stay for as long as you need.' I just about managed to nod in response.

This had to go above and beyond a park ranger's job description, but somehow his kindness made it even harder to stem the tears that were coursing down my cheeks. He didn't push me about what was wrong, though, and we walked in silence, except for the occasional half-sob that bubbled to the surface no matter how hard I tried to swallow them down.

Harry was true to his word, and he found me an empty office to sit in in the Ranger's Center, while he made the drinks. My head was pounding, and I probably looked even worse than I felt. It had been almost two years, but something unexpected could still take me back to the same blindsiding level of pain I'd felt in the moment I found out about the accident. Anything could trigger it, but I suppose I shouldn't have been surprised that it would happen here.

Harry returned with two steaming mugs of coffee and passed one to me. 'I can leave you on your own,' he said, then hesitated, his dark brown eyes suddenly anxious. 'Unless you'd like some company? It might help to talk about it?'

I put my hands around the cup, warmth seeping into my skin. For some reason, I felt like I owed Harry an explanation; he was being so lovely and there was something about him that made me want to open up and talk. I never really did that, not even with my closest friends, but I semed as powerless to stop the words as I had been to stop the tears. 'I... lost my parents and, I don't know, the plaque just hit a nerve.'

'I'm so sorry.' His voice was gentle.

'It happened nearly two years ago, and I wanted to punch people in the early days, when they said the pain would ease with time. Now I just want to tell them that they're liars.'

'I don't think you ever truly get over losing someone you love.' By now, Harry was probably wishing he'd just walked me out to the edge of the park. But maybe he was right. Maybe I did need to talk about it, even though I knew it wouldn't change anything.

'It's even worse because I feel like all of this is all my fault.'

His brows furrowed slightly. 'What do you mean it was your fault?' For all he knew, I was a serial killer, and he was locked in an empty office with me. No wonder he looked uneasy. I'd have to tell him the whole story.

'I booked them a trip to New York for my mum's fiftieth birthday, but there was a crash on the way to the airport and...' Even after all this time, I still struggled to say the words. 'They were both killed instantly.'

'You were driving?' Harry didn't wait for an answer and he put his hands over mine. It should have been uncomfortably over-familiar, but it wasn't. 'Just because you were driving, it doesn't make it your fault. It was a terrible accident, that's all.'

'I wasn't driving. Dad was.' I tried not to picture the mangled wreckage that was all that had been left of their car. I'd seen photographs at the trial, and I hadn't been able to get the images out of my head since. 'They were pushed into the wrong lane, by another driver overtaking on a blind bend, and they hit a lorry head-on.'

'How can any of that be *your* fault?' It was an echo of the words I'd heard so many times – from well-meaning friends, my grandparents, and even my counsellor, but the guilt still ate away at me. I'd put them on that road, at that time. Maybe if I hadn't been so busy at work, and I'd offered to drive them, they'd still be here. I might have reacted differently to Dad, and somehow avoided the crash altogether. Or maybe I'd have died with them. I didn't want that any more – not like I had in the beginning – but it still felt like the easier option sometimes.

'I booked the trip, and I chose a flight time that meant they were travelling on a dark road, in the winter. If it hadn't been icy and almost pitch black, maybe Dad could have steered clear of the lorry.'

'What about the person who was overtaking? Surely they were the one to blame?'

'It was pretty clear he'd been taking drugs and probably drinking too, just hours before the accident. But he played up his injuries at the hospital and was taken for an emergency scan; the delay in testing was long enough for the tests to come back inconclusive. By the time they were taken, he was just under the legal limit for both TCH and alcohol.' I'd learnt the true meaning of hate, when I'd seen the police report on what that man had done and the background to his previous driving charges. I wasn't stupid, I knew it was his fault, but I still felt I was somehow to blame too. The guilt I felt for booking my parents night flights, just to save a couple of hundred pounds, would stay with me forever. It was money I could have stretched to, but the consequences were so final. And no amount of 'what ifs' did any good – they just piled on the pain.

'Libby, you've got to stop blaming yourself.' Harry hesitated again, and I wanted to tell him that he didn't need to try and help me, because plenty of professionals before him had tried and failed. But it was like he could read my mind. 'I'm sure you've had threapy to try and work through all this, but I've got this friend...'

'Please tell me it's not a psychic!' I cut him off. I'd had all sorts of suggestions since I'd lost my parents, and I'd very nearly gone that far. But I didn't believe in any of that. It would have done just as much as the counselling seemed to do, and the well-intentioned platitudes of friends that didn't help either. All I could do was hope that time would eventually make it a little bit easier to live with, because nothing else had and I'd realised pretty quickly that 'getting over' my parents' deaths was never going to happen.

'No, of course not. Look, I'm sorry, this is probably overstepping the mark, but I've seen her do amazing work with people going through the process of grief. She specialises in art rehabilitation and she works out of the Community Center about half a mile from your aunt's shop. It's not therapy as such, it's just using art as a way of getting you to open up. Maybe it'd be worth a try?' Harry took a card out of his wallet and handed it to me.

'Dr Paula?' She sounded like one of those therapists on daytime talk-show phone-ins, offering advice to 'anonymous from Milton Keynes', on the unexplained rash that had appeared after an encounter with a stranger.

'She's great, I promise, and she does her art rehabilitation work pro bono. You just make a donation to the Community Center she works out of, if you can afford it. She might be able to help, and what have you got to lose?'

'Nothing I suppose.' I'd already lost everything, so there'd be no harm in giving it a go. But shoving the card into my coat pocket, I had no real intention of ever visiting Dr Paula's art class. Fate, it seemed, had other ideas.

4

'My therapist says I've got to break the cycle.' Madison was threading red and green ribbon around a huge wreath in the shop window as she spoke. It was after closing time, but there was still a long list of things Aunt Dottie wanted us to get through. 'She said I'll just spend my life going from one loser to the next, otherwise.'

'Wow, how old are you again?' I'd like to have given Madison's therapist some advice of my own. She shouldn't be fixating on men of any kind to sort her life out, she should be out enjoying herself. But then I was a fine one to talk about living life.

'I was twenty last month and I can't go on like this.' Madison shook her head, as if she thought time really was running out for her and I had to suppress the urge to laugh. I might only be a decade or so older than her, but it could be a million years for the difference it made and the very last thing on my mind was focusing on finding a partner. Maybe it wasn't the number of years that separated us, maybe it was the things that had happened.

I looked across at Betty, who rolled her eyes. 'When I moved up here from Georgia, I didn't know a soul until I met my first husband. And I was so grateful to him for providing for me. He spent half his life making sure I knew how lucky I was supposed to feel, too. I was so convinced that he was right, I put up with his womanising and drinking for years. Trust me, you don't ever want to be reliant on a man, sugar. You gotta make your own way in the world.' Betty had taken the words right out of my mouth, but, unlike me, she could speak from experience.

'And is this what you want to do, Madison, work in a Christmas shop?' Aunt Dottie would probably kill me if she could hear me. She'd already said that good staff like Madison were hard to find, but I couldn't help wondering why a young girl like her didn't want more out of life. I could see the appeal for Betty, and even for Madison if she ever actually got to run the place and do things her way. But I couldn't see Dottie ever handing over the reins.

'I'm gonna go to college eventually – I'd like to teach in an elementary school – but my mom raised me on her own, so there was never any college fund to rely on. I'm supposed to be saving up while I'm working, but there's always something to pay for. Thank God my insurance covers the therapy, or I'd never get anything saved.'

'I already told you what you should do, sugar; it worked for my grandson, Tyrell.' Betty was back behind the counter, packaging up mail-order decorations for delivery. She was like a machine. I'd never seen anyone wrap brown paper parcels so fast. 'He started at the community college and got half his degree. It saved him thousands of dollars.'

'I know, Betty, and I'm gonna register next year, I promise.' Madison didn't look up from attaching baubles to the wreath. 'But I've still gotta get my head straight when it comes to guys. My therapist reckons it's all down to my dad coming in and out of my life so much when I was a kid, then disappearing altogether. She recommended I go to an art class at the Community Center on the corner of Tenth and Sixty-First. It's on tonight, but I really don't think it's my kinda thing.'

My ears pricked up at this and I couldn't help but flush as my mind went back to the conversation I'd had with Harry in Central Park. I couldn't believe I'd said so much, and to a stranger, too. I'd have to wear a balaclava the next time I went to the park – I couldn't face seeing him again. Ever. I hadn't even been as honest with my grandparents as I'd been with Harry and I still had no idea why I'd done it. At first, I'd felt a bit better about finally getting it off my chest with someone who wasn't paid to listen, or to tell me it hadn't been my fault. Maybe I'd even believed it for a little while, because when I'd headed back through the park it had been like some of the weight had finally lifted off my shoulders. I'd even laughed, really laughed, for the first time in what felt like forever, when I'd walked past a police car that had looked so different from every depiction of a New York police car I'd ever seen on TV or in a movie. It was tiny, almost like a clown's car. I couldn't resist taking a snap of it and I was still laughing to myself when I got back to the apartment above the shop. But then I'd thought about how the one person I wanted to share the picture with was gone, and the lightness I'd felt as a result of opening up to Harry had disappeared instantly. I was back to square one and not sure I'd ever find a way to move forward.

'And how are my three favourite shop girls today?' Dannie charged through the door of Candy Cane Lane, ignoring the closed sign, with Rob following on right behind him. 'You're going to love us, we've got cheesecake!'

'Sugar, you read my mind!' Betty put down the tape gun, and lifted the corner of the box that Rob had put down on the counter, along with some paper plates and wooden forks. 'Peanut butter and banana! I swear, if I wasn't already married, Rob, I would make you an offer you *could not* refuse!'

'I would find it very difficult, Betty. Although Dannie might have something to say about it.' Rob cut her a large slice of cheesecake.

'Oh, I don't know.' Dannie grinned. 'I'd be willing to swap him for your jerk chicken recipe, Betty. What do you think, have we got a deal?'

'You know I've promised to leave you that in my will, Dannie.' Betty smacked her lips as she put a forkful of cheesecake into her mouth. 'Although, I might be willing to betray my Jamaican roots, and my husband, for a man who can make cheesecake this good.'

'So, what's the gossip?' Dannie looked from Madison to me, and back again.

'We were just talking about the advice my therapist gave me.' Stepping out of the window display, Madison took a piece of cheesecake from Rob.

'Now this sounds like it's about to get juicy!' Dannie picked up the Swarovski crystal bauble again, and Rob shook his head. It looked like a battle that was going to last until Christmas Day.

'Not really. She wants me to go to a special art class at the Community Center tonight, to help me work through my issues with men.' Madison wrinkled her nose.

'With Dr Paula?' Dannie looked even more excited. 'Apparently she's fab. We've been thinking about trying the classes for ages. And Rob's sister runs the Community Center that Dr Paula runs her classes out of. Doesn't she, Rob?'

'Yeah, Karly's worked there for a few years now. They do all sorts of stuff – they've even got a theatre group that performs there, too. They used to run some off-Broadway shows there, but now it's mainly a meeting place with workshops, community classes and a bit of alternative theatre.'

'Ooh, you know what? We should all go!' Dannie was a force to be reckoned with, and I tried to back into the corner of the shop, in the hope he wouldn't remember I was there. 'We've got staff in covering the deli until it closes, so we could go tonight.'

'You got some issues you need to work through, too, sugar?' Betty was using her wrapping skills to pack up another two slices of cheesecake. That woman was nobody's fool.

'We've all got issues, chicken.' Dannie grinned again. 'But I've always fancied myself as a bit of an artist. I could do a mural for the deli if I get really good.'

'Or you could spend the whole evening finding out what everyone else's issues are?' Rob raised an eyebrow, and I was more determined than ever to dodge going with them. I'd already told a complete stranger much more than I wanted to. But I definitely didn't want my neighbours and colleagues knowing what a mess I was – they were people I'd have to face every day.

'So it's settled then, we're going to tonight's class?' Dannie looked around, but Betty was already packing up her handbag.

'I've gotta get home to Jacob, but I think it's a great idea that you're taking Madison. And it will be good for Libby to meet some more people, too. I know that's what her Aunt Dottie wants.' She fixed me with an uncharacteristically serious look, and I wondered how much my great aunt had already told her. Everything, knowing Dottie.

'That's settled then; Rob can give his sister a call.' Dannie put an arm around Madison, who didn't look much more convinced than me. At least we could try and brazen it out together. Making a joke of the whole thing would certainly lessen the chance of anyone discovering who I really was.

'I'm not sure Libby wants to be railroaded into this.' Rob turned to look at me, and I could see the sympathy in his eyes. I had a horrible feeling that I'd been right, when I'd first met the boys, and that Betty wasn't the only one Aunt Dottie had been talking to. She'd probably done it with the best of intentions. But, apart from not being in Canterbury when Grant Bailey came home on a visit, being able to reinvent myself, even for a little while, had been one of the things that had appealed to me most about spending two months in New York. I didn't want to be the woman who'd lost both her parents in a horrific accident. Only now, it looked increasingly like that might be the only thing anyone in this part of Manhattan knew about me.

'It's fine, it'll probably be a laugh.' It didn't sound convincing, even to me. But I was going anyway, because I couldn't stand the looks they'd exchange otherwise. 'Poor Libby' was a label I wasn't prepared to wear, at least not here, and I owed it to my parents to embrace the chances they'd never been given. The only way to stand any chance of doing that was to fake it until I made it and pretend I could handle it all – Christmas, New York and now art classes with Dr Paula.

* * *

The Community Center was much nicer than I expected, and there were paintings on the outside of the building. It had pretty leaded windows, too, edged with red and green glass, which gave it a really Christmassy feel. But I tried not to let that put me off. It must have been quite grand in its heyday, but it was attached to a dilapidated building that only seemed to have one wall left standing. There were still posters on it, though, which must have been there for decades, advertising Broadway shows that had long since closed.

Madison looked like she was going to a nightclub, in her tiny little crop top and skin-tight jeans. Not that I was jealous. But, when I looked at her, I tried to suck my stomach in anyway – two slices of Rob's peanut butter and banana cheesecake weren't helping. Despite knowing there were probably half a day's calories in each slice, part of me was glad I'd wanted another slice. After my parents had died, I'd had no appetite for weeks and when I'd forced myself to eat – mostly to stop my grandparents worrying – everything had tasted like sand. One of the things Dad had most been looking forward to about coming to New York was visiting as many delis as he could get to. He loved watching programmes like *Man v. Food* and had told me he wasn't coming home until he'd won at least one food challenge and got the T-shirt to prove it. He'd have been in his version of heaven in Dannie and Rob's deli and I'd almost been able to picture him standing beside me, when I'd considered having a second slice of the cheesecake they'd dropped off, urging me to do it. Dad definitely wouldn't have held back and I told myself I was having the second slice for him.

'I'm so glad you finally came!' A pretty girl, who I could only assume was Rob's sister, greeted us as soon as we walked through the door.

'It was all Dannie's idea.' Rob offered the introductions. 'This is Madison and Libby, they run Candy Cane Lane. You know, the Christmas shop next to the deli.'

'Ooh I *love* that place!' I could see why Karly had been given the job of running the Community Center; she had the knack of making you feel immediately at home and a ready smile that somehow convinced me on the spot that she was someone I would get on with. 'I'm so glad you're all here, and I've told Paula to expect you, so, you can head through to the studio when you're ready. But Abbie will kill me if I don't give you these first. It's her new show.' She passed us all a black-and-white leaflet, with a picture of a woman on the front, whose head was covered with a white sheet wrapped in barbed wire.

'Looks cheerful.' Rob turned over the leaflet. 'Oh damn, I think we're busy that week, aren't we, Dannie?'

'Don't be mean.' Karly nudged her brother. 'The ticket sales go towards keeping this place running. So, even if you don't think it's your thing, you should give it a go. For me.'

'How about if we pay not to go?' Dannie laughed and looked at me. 'But, hey, Libby's never experienced Abbie's theatre group before, and she could be into performance art for all we know.'

'And I thought you said us Brits had to stick together.' I put the leaflet into my bag. Maybe I should give it a go. At least I'd have plenty to talk about when I got back to my grandparents' pub. I could just imagine the regulars' reactions, when I told them about it, and Nan wouldn't be able to say I hadn't got out and about. When I called her, I'd be able to say I'd started art classes with friends, and booked to go to the theatre. That had to count as having a life. Maybe after that I'd be able to go to a Broadway show too. That was something else on Mum's wish list and Dad had secretly booked tickets to see *Chicago* on the second night of their stay, despite pretending to protest about the idea of going to the theatre. She'd have been thrilled and, even if there was no way I could follow their plans closely enough to go to the same show, without having a complete breakdown and ugly crying all the way through, it was something else I wanted to do for Mum before I left.

'Come on then, let's get up to the studio, so I can release my inner Picasso.' Dannie's voice broke into my thoughts and he was already walking away. 'See you later, Karls, and get the kettle on for after. You've got some Yorkshire tea in, haven't you?'

'I certainly have! I know it's more than my life's worth not to have what it takes to make a proper brew, as you call it. Before I met you, I never realised Yorkshiremen were so particular about tea! Have fun guys and I'll see you afterwards.' Karly turned and headed back towards the reception area, where four pugs were lying on a leather sofa. They were so still, they could have passed for statues – apart from the snoring.

* * *

'Come in, come in!' A woman in a wheelchair, at the front of the art studio, waved us in. She had amazing blue eyes, and I immediately felt as though she could see into my soul. Maybe that was why her classes had such a great reputation: she really could see beyond the surface. I wondered if it was too late to make a bolt for it, because I really didn't want her to be able to do that with me. 'I'm Paula, and I would say I run these classes, but they tend to run themselves. But I do make sure that no one steals the supplies, and I try to be a listening ear if you need one. I don't provide directed therapy at these sessions, though. So, if you're looking for a traditional art therapy class, I can recommend some other places. I'm guessing you're the group of friends Karly told me about?'

We all introduced ourselves in turn and, within minutes, Madison was pouring out her boyfriend troubles to Paula as the rest of the group gradually drifted into the studio. There were others already working on projects and some of them were amazing, although there was a good chance that a couple of them would end up giving me nightmares. One man was doing what I can only assume was a self-portrait. The face was recognisable, but it was attached to the body of a baby that was wearing a nappy. It made me shudder just looking at it and I had no desire to find out the meaning behind it. Despite the sinister nature of some of the artwork, there was a really relaxed atmosphere and Paula's unobtrusive approach seemed to work like magic in getting people to open up. Not for me, though. I was busy concentrating on doing a very bad painting of a dog instead, inspired by Karly's pugs. I might not have been working through my issues, but I had managed to unleash my inner five-year-old, judging by the quality of my artwork.

'I didn't think you'd actually join the class. You looked pretty unconvinced when I gave you the card.' My brush slipped when I realised who was speaking. Harry must have come into the studio while I was engrossed in my painting. If it wasn't embarrassing enough that I'd cried all over his office, now he could see my pitiful attempt at painting, too. So much for trying to avoid seeing him again.

'I wasn't, to be honest, but some friends persuaded me. I'm only here to support Madison, really.' I was going to have to get better at this nonchalant stuff. I just sounded whiney.

'That's what we all say at first.' Harry smiled and bent down to kiss Paula on the cheek when she came over. So that explained how keen he'd been to give me her card – they were clearly a couple, which meant Paula probably knew my innermost secrets too.

'I hope this guy isn't bothering you?' Paula laughed, and I shook my head. Something about Harry *did* bother me, but not for the reason she meant. I still felt as if I'd met him before – it had to be that he reminded me of someone else, but I just couldn't place who. That had to explain why I felt so jittery around him; I hated not being able to work out what caused the jolt of recognition every time I saw him.

'No, he's not bothering me. Harry was the one who recommended your class.'

'Ah, maybe I should put him on commission. Although 10 per cent of nothing is still nothing.' Paula glanced down at my drawing, and I fought the urge to cover it up with my arms – like a child trying to stop the kid next to her from copying her work. Although no one in their right mind would want to copy my artwork. 'That's very interesting.'

'What? Interesting how bad it is! It's just a really terrible drawing of one of the dogs I saw downstairs.' Let her try and make something deep and meaningful out of that. Even if Harry had told her what had happened to my parents, I felt pretty certain there was nothing in the drawing that she could link to it.

'It's not so much the dog, it's the house in the background.' Paula leant forward in her wheelchair, and pointed to the tiny house I'd drawn, as if it was miles away from the dog. 'Why is the house so far in the distance?'

'I was just filling up the empty space.'

'But there's still lots of empty space; you could have filled much more of it by drawing the house closer to the dog.' She looked at me without saying anything, her gaze so intense that in the end I was desperate to fill the silence.

'He's lost.' I hadn't wanted to admit that was what I was thinking, when I'd drawn the dog. It didn't mean anything. It was just that my attempt at drawing the pug's squishy little face had left him looking sad, that was all.

'Definitely interesting.' Paula glanced at Harry, and then back at me. 'We can talk later, if you like.'

I was tempted to say that I was sure Harry had already blabbed everything there was to know about my emotional state of mind. But I didn't want to cry in front of Harry again, or anyone else for that matter, so I just nodded.

When they moved off to the other side of the studio, I couldn't get back into my painting. I didn't want to give Paula any more ammunition to find hidden meaning. It was just a dog, for God's sake.

Unlike me, Madison, Dannie and Rob all seemed to be really into what they were doing, so I wandered around the studio, trying to avoid looking at what anyone else was painting. I didn't want to see if there had been any more additions to the man-baby, or to start interpreting clouds on someone else's painting as representing the inner turmoil of the human mind. Or, worse still, to discover that I was the only one who sucked at painting. There were lots of pictures up on the walls, but there was one I kept being drawn back to. I couldn't take my eyes of it.

'It's awesome, isn't it?' Harry had snuck up on me again. The man really ought to come with a warning.

'It's beautiful.' It was like a kaleidoscope of colour, and the design made it look as if there was no end to it. I'd never seen anything like it before. 'Are these all done by members of the art group?' I felt more ashamed of my lonely pug than ever.

'No, Paula runs a straight-up art class too. As well as teaching some psychology classes at NYU and seeing private clients out of her offices on Sixth.' It made me tired just listening to how much she did, but the pride in Harry's voice was obvious. He clearly loved her and who wouldn't want to be with someone who radiated energy the way she did. When he'd stood next to us, it must have been like standing with Tigger and Eeyore. For some reason I wanted to know more about their lives together, even though picturing them as a couple suddenly made it hard to swallow.

'Busy lady. That must make it difficult for you two to make time to see each other.'

'Yeah, sometimes it does.' He gave me a strange look. Funny how he didn't like it when it was turned on him – having someone probing into *his* personal life. Well two could play at that game and I needed to really be able to imagine their lives together, so I could stop wondering what it might be like to kiss him when I watched his mouth as he spoke.

'Have you known each other long?'

'We met at college.' Harry turned back to the painting, cutting off my line of questioning. 'This is one of DeShawn's paintings. Paula can't work out why he keeps coming back to her class, when there's nothing she can teach someone that talented. But I have a pretty good idea.'

I looked at the signature on the painting. Whoever DeShawn Parshall was, I admired Harry's lack of jealousy. It was obvious the guy was going to Paula's classes just to see her, and Harry knew it too.

'I don't know about you, chicken, but I am *so* ready for a proper brew. This being an artistic genius is much more tiring than it looks.' Dannie came over to where we were standing. 'What about you, Harry, are you going to join us?'

'You two know each other?' So much for big cities being anonymous.

'I told you that, remember.' Harry paused. 'When we spoke in the park.'

'Ah, I was wondering how *you two* knew each other!' Dannie tapped the side of his nose. 'Well Paula said she'd join us, and Rob's brought some blueberry swirl cheesecake.'

I'd have liked to say that the thought of a third slice of cheesecake in one day didn't appeal, but that would have been a lie. I'd definitely have to join the joggers in the park at this rate, but I was determined to hang on to the positives. Rob's cheesecakes tasted of paradise and, after all, I was doing this for Dad.

'Only an idiot would turn that down.' Harry smiled at me, and suddenly a crazy thought went through my head: I wish I'd met him at a different time, when he didn't have a brilliant and beautiful girlfriend, and I didn't have enough emotional baggage to fill Grand Central Station. The thought took me by surprise. It was the first time since my parents had died that I'd needed to remind myself the barriers I'd put up were there to protect me. Maybe it was just the magic of being in New York. I was already doing so many things I'd never have dreamt of doing back in Canterbury. Whatever feelings were being stirred up every time I looked at Harry's mouth and imagined what it would be like to kiss him would pass and, even if they didn't, I'd be going home before I knew it and I'd forget all about him before I even landed in Heathrow.

* * *

'Yorkshire tea and New York cheesecake; if that isn't the perfect fusion of two cultures, I don't know what is.' Karly put the cheese-cake in the middle of the table in the Community Center café, which had a small bar at one end. 'It doesn't matter how many times you stare at me, guys, you aren't getting any cheesecake.' She looked down at the pugs, who were following her every move with their eyes.

'Aw, poor old Olly and George – you're such a meany. As for Lola and Gladys, how can you resist those faces?' Dannie bent down and patted each of the pugs on the top of their heads in turn. Four pugs breathing excitedly made it sound a bit like a steam train was heading in our direction, but despite the sound, I couldn't help but wonder whether having an animal to care for could work for me as well; they certainly seemed to make Karly happy. I'd been thinking about getting a dog for a while; the only thing that put me off was the fact that they had such short lives. Letting myself love an animal and having to face the prospect of one day losing it, had stopped me from acting on my plans. Although what Karly said next put me off a bit too.

'Listen, these four virtually push me out of my own bed at night and they get plenty of treats, just not cheesecake.' She sat down at the table with everyone else. 'They already leak more hot air than a Con Ed steam pipe as it is!'

'A what?' I had no idea if I'd even heard her right and I instinc-tively looked across at Harry for clarification.

'They're the orange and white pipes you see on the roads; they release the steam from the heating systems in the buildings.' He smiled. 'It paints quite the picture of the dogs' gas problem, doesn't it?'

'It certainly does.' I returned his smile as the conversation amongst the group continued. It wasn't just Harry I felt an unexplained connection with. It was strange how at home I felt with these people who I'd only known for days, hours in Paula's case – but they already felt like friends. Maybe it was because I'd spent all my time with my grandparents' friends over the last couple of years, feeling like a spare part and knowing they all felt sorry for me. Whatever the reason, I'd forgotten how much fun just chatting could be and it had been worth coming to the art class for that alone.

'I'm glad you're all still here!' A girl who looked like she was in her mid-twenties came into the café, and you could almost feel the energy coming off her. Looking to my right, I saw Rob slide down in his seat.

'Abbie, this is Libby and Madison. I think you're the only ones who haven't met.' Karly pulled a chair out for Abbie as she spoke, but the younger girl didn't take it. It was almost as if she had too much energy to sit down.

'Nice to meet you!' She looked around the table. 'So, how many tickets should I put you all down for? Karly said she gave you the info.'

'Is the play going to be as weird as the flyers make it look?' Paula said what everyone else was almost certainly thinking and I had to fight to stop the corners of my mouth from turning up the way they were so desperate to do.

'Do you want to end up having to look for somewhere else to run your colouring-in classes?' It turned out that Abbie could give as good as she got, and they both laughed. 'Come on, people, all the funds are going to keeping this place open, and keeping these pugs in the lifestyle they've gotten accustomed to. Where else is

Karly gonna find a job where they let her take the four dogs in to sleep on the couch all day? This is an important cause, and you're not getting out of it. That includes you, Rob.'

'As if I'd miss a play about' – Rob picked up one of the flyers – 'the emancipation of millennial woman.'

'What about you, Libby? Are you up for experiencing some off-off-Broadway avant-garde theatre?' Harry's dark eyes twinkled and, if I hadn't known better, I'd have sworn he was flirting with me. I shot a furtive glance towards Paula, but she didn't seem at all bothered. She obviously had as much trust in him as he did in her.

'Well, if everyone else is going...?' Okay, maybe a play about the liberation of modern women was never going to be top of my New York wish list, even if it was a stepping stone to being able to watch a Broadway show without Mum by my side. But, despite my doubts, I'd had a great evening at the art class, so I was willing to give it a go. And one thing was for certain, I was learning to make friends again, which had to be a step in the right direction.

'That's settled then.' Abbie finally sat down and helped herself to the last slice of cheesecake.

'You have no idea what you've got us into,' Dannie whispered into my ear as Abbie started handing out the tickets, 'but you definitely owe me that Swarovski bauble now.'

I caught Harry's eye again. Seeing the show would give me another chance to work out why I was hit by déjà vu every time he looked in my direction, and I'd have been happy to part with a dozen Swarovski baubles for that.

5

Aunt Dottie was only just over five-feet tall, but she seemed to take up half the shop when she was in there. By the third week of November, she'd managed to ditch the scooter and was walking with a stick. She still wasn't up to working a full shift in the shop, but that didn't stop her popping in on a regular basis to check up on us.

'So how are the fall lines selling? It's only a week to Thanksgiving, so we've got to shift as much of it as we can.' Dottie wasn't telling us anything we didn't already know. One wall of the shop was decorated with the range from the fall line, with hessian bunting spelling out 'Happy Thanksgiving', tea-light holders with orange glass, and wreaths decorated with dried flowers and miniature pumpkins.

'We've sold about three quarters of the stock.' If I'd expected a pat on the back from my great aunt, I was in for a disappointment.

'Well then, you need to keep pushing it hard over the next few days. No one who comes in here for a Christmas decoration should leave without something from the fall line too.' Now I knew how she'd managed to keep a shop running on Seventh

Avenue. This was no location for the faint-hearted, and I knew how much needed to go through the till, just to cover overheads.

'We'll give it our best shot, won't we Madison?'

'Of course. We always do.' She was making her second attempt at sticking together a gingerbread house, but it already had more frosting than gingerbread on it, and I didn't think any amount of extra icing could salvage it. We had a stack of gingerbread-house kits to sell, too. And we had to put one together to show customers what it would be like, but these things were always more difficult than they looked and not even *DIY SOS* could have salvaged this place.

'How are things with Brian?' It was time for a change of subject, and Aunt Dottie's face lit up when I mentioned his name.

'Very good, actually. It was Brian who suggested I go for a fall colour in time for Thanksgiving.' Dottie patted her hair. It wasn't quite pumpkin-orange, but 'vibrant' would have been an understatement.

'It's striking.' I caught Madison's eye and had to glance down at the order book for a minute to stop my face from giving me away. I loved the fact that I'd wanted to laugh so much more since I'd arrived in New York, but it could have its downsides. 'We've had a lot of big orders in, since we started the shipping service.' I'd suggested offering to ship ornaments back to customers' home countries, during the first week I was working in the shop. We already offered online mail order for some of our lines in the US, so it seemed like a natural extension of the service. People were definitely willing to order more, once they were sure they could get it home safely and not open their suitcases to discover the beautiful glass bauble they'd bought, as a memento of New York, had been shattered into a thousand pieces.

'It was a good idea, I suppose.' Dottie's praise might have been grudging, but it meant all the more because of that. No one could describe her as gushing – if she paid you a compliment, she meant it and that was quite something.

A group of French tourists came into the shop, and Aunt Dottie mouthed the words 'fall line' in a really over-exaggerated way. I didn't rate our chances of selling much of the Thanksgiving merchandise to people who didn't even celebrate it, but I was willing to give it a go.

'I'll see you later then, girls.' Aunt Dottie squeezed past the customers as I went over to see if they needed any help. 'Brian's promised me a neck and shoulder massage, and I wouldn't want to be late for that little treat!'

Hoping our French customers didn't speak good enough English to pick up on how loaded with innuendo Aunt Dottie's words were, I watched her go outside and hail a cab like a pro. Smiling to myself, I wondered if I'd have half her chutzpah when I was in my seventies, and then I felt that twist in my stomach again – my parents hadn't even made it out of their fifties alive. What right did I have to imagine an old age, when they'd been robbed of theirs?

* * *

I hadn't expected to see Auntie Dottie again that day. Usually when she had a date with Brian, for a neck and shoulder massage, or anything else for that matter, she didn't make a reappearance. So, when I saw a flash of orange hair as she came back into the shop, just as I was finishing closing up, I was almost as surprised as I'd been about how many items from the fall line I'd managed to sell to our French customers in the end.

'Oh hello, I didn't think you be back in again today. Is everything okay?' I looked at my great aunt, who had an uncharacteristically serious expression on her face.

'Where's Madison? I need to tell you something.' Aunt Dottie scanned the room, as if she expected Madison to suddenly jump out from behind one of the display racks, and panic rose in my throat. If something had happened to my grandparents... My breath was coming in short rasps and my chest had gone tight, but somehow I managed to get two words out.

'Gone home.'

'Good.' Auntie Dottie's expression immediately relaxed and it felt as if all the air had left my body. 'Are you okay, kid? You've gone a real funny colour.'

'I'm fine, I just thought when you said you needed to tell me something, that maybe there'd been another...' I couldn't finish the sentence, but my aunt seemed to understand.

'Oh honey, I'm so sorry, I should have thought. It's okay, it's nothing bad.' Aunt Dottie enveloped me in a hug and I could have stayed there forever, because if felt so much like one of Nan's cuddles. She even smelled the same, with the scent of lily of the valley clinging to her even more closely than I was. If the traces of Youth Dew on the dressing gown belonged to her, she certainly wasn't wearing that perfume now.

'No, it's me. I'm just being silly. My mind always seems to go to the worst-case scenario these days. I wish it didn't, but it does.' I gave her a watery smile as I pulled away. 'I told Maddison to go when most of the closing up was done; I was just finishing up and you'll be pleased to hear we've now sold 90 per cent of the fall stock. I think there are still a few online orders to process, too. Rush delivery as well, so you can charge extra.'

'Now you're talking my kind of language!' Aunt Dottie winked and I felt a strange sensation, as if I'd found the place where I truly belonged. It was quickly followed by a rush of guilt. I couldn't possibly feel like I belonged in New York when my grandparents were in Canterbury, with my parents' ashes buried in the church-yard just a few minutes' walk from their house.

'I knew you'd be pleased,' I said, internally shaking myself and forcing my thoughts back to the matter at hand. 'Now, what was it you wanted to tell me?' I was holding my breath again, but this time it was for a very different reason. Crossing my fingers over one another, I was just hoping that whatever my aunt wanted to confide, it wouldn't have anything to do with Brian or his alleged ability to give the best massage in Manhattan.

'I wanted to tell you that it's okay to be happy again.' Aunt Dottie's eyes never left my face. 'I recognise that look you get when you catch yourself smiling. I saw you do it this morning.'

'Do what?'

'Stop in the middle of something that makes you happy and then wait until the smile has slid right off your face.' She grabbed hold of my hand. 'You don't have to deny yourself that. I understand how hard it is to lose someone you love, but the last thing your parents would want is for you to be unhappy.'

I shook my head. 'I know you and Nan lost your dad when you were really young and that must have been tough, but it wasn't the same. You couldn't have done anything about that.' Until I met Harry, I'd never admitted to anyone that part of me blamed myself for Mum and Dad's accident, but now I didn't seem able to stop admitting it.

'And you think there's something you could have done to prevent their accident?' Aunt Dottie raised her eyebrows. 'You're going to have to tell me how the hell you came up with that, when it was all down to that waste of air they locked up for it.'

I could have told Aunt Dottie the same things I'd said to Harry, about feeling guilty because it was my choice of flight time that had put them in Grant Bailey's path. Or how things might have been different if I'd taken a day off work to drive them to the airport, so it was me behind the wheel when the accident happened. But it wasn't even about that any more. Since I'd spoken to Harry, some of the guilt about those things finally seemed to have eased. I knew no one in their right mind could really blame me for the accident, not even me, but feeling better about that made me feel even worse about not getting my parents the justice they deserved. Their accident was the fault of a man whose name my aunt couldn't even bear to use, but I'd let him get away with it.

'It's not just the accident, it's the fact I didn't fight hard enough to make sure Grant Bailey got the sentence he should have done.'

'From what I heard, you barely ate or slept trying to make that happen, but sometimes life isn't fair. In fact, sometimes it sucks.'

She wasn't wrong. After the accident, I'd researched every case I could, convinced it would help determine the outcome of Bailey's trial, but it didn't make a shred of difference in the end. 'I can't help thinking that if I'd just tried a bit harder, things might not have worked out the way they did.'

She shook her head. 'This is what Ruby was most scared of, that you'd end up living to get revenge on that scumbag, knowing that no sentence would ever take away the emptiness you felt. You need to find something else to fill that space. That's why she wanted you to come here.'

'I know.' Nan was a wise woman and I'd started to lose some of that hollowed out feeling since I'd arrived in New York, but it wouldn't last forever. 'It's just I can't help thinking when I go home it'll all—'

'One step at a time.' Aunt Dottie cut me off. 'Let this city show you what life has to offer and then you can start worrying about how you hold on to that feeling once you're home. That's why I came back here, to take you out.'

'You're taking me out?'

'You betcha and we've got to be there in twenty minutes.'

'Where are we going?'

'That would be telling.' Dottie tapped the side of her nose. 'But if you're not already wearing pants with some give at the waist, you might want to think about changing.'

'I need to wear bigger pants?' My eyes widened and Aunt Dottie laughed.

'I forget these days that you call them trousers.' Aunt Dottie dropped the perfect wink. 'Come on then, you've got ten minutes before the cab gets here and by the time we're done, you'll forget what it's like to be a Brit too!'

* * *

True to her word, Dottie had found a way to immerse me in all that New York had to offer and she'd been spot on about the need for a loose waistband too. All the arrangements had been made so that her mobility issues didn't curtail the plans and I'd never seen the inside of so many taxi cabs in a single night. If I'd needed a reminder of how many people chose to start a new life in New York, just chatting to some of the drivers would have been an education in itself. Dottie's beloved city was the home of fresh starts, and I was about to discover parts of it I'd almost certainly never have seen without her.

First stop had been a doughnut tour. I couldn't believe anyone had thought to come up with it, or that there were so many ways to eat them. I knew my aunt had a passion for doughnuts and she'd regularly turn up with Krispy Kremes when she came into the shop. There were always at least two missing from the box of a dozen, which she jokingly called her delivery tax. But I still hadn't expected her to be the sommelier of the doughnut world.

'You can taste the lemon they put in the batter for this one, can't you?' Aunt Dottie had closed her eyes to savour the flavour and I'd nearly choked laughing. All I knew was that I'd never tasted a better sugared doughnut. Then there'd been all the flavoured ones, everything from peanut butter and banana to passion fruit and coconut.

After the tour was over, when all I'd wanted to do was to lie down and undo the top button of my trousers, Dottie had other plans. That was how I'd found myself in a bar in Greenwich Village, listening to the blues and feeling as if every song had been written for me. Maybe it was working my way through the whiskey, bourbon and rye that my aunt insisted we absolutely had to try, but after three drinks, something shifted in me as I looked around the bar.

Everyone in there seemed to be having the same experience, feeling the music on a deeper level than I ever had before, and then it hit me. Every single person in the room had been through something that made the lyrics meaningful to *them*. There was one song that really got to me. It was about a man losing his wife and the loss making him realise he had to live for the two of them. It seemed to capture the shift that had happened since I'd arrived in New York. I'd started off still wrapped up in the guilt that I'd worn like a cloak since the accident, feeling terrible for being in the city my mother had always dreamed of visiting when she never would. But listening to the song, I realised that just lately I'd started doing what the lyrics suggested: living my life for the three of us. Nan had been right about me coming here, like she was about so many things. Aunt Dottie had clearly understood that long before I did, but she'd found a way to finally make me realise.

'So what do you think, the perfect night out or what?' She nudged me as we sat side by side in the taxicab that was weaving its way back through the streets of Manhattan.

'It couldn't have been better.'

'I think you might be right, and you look really different.' Dottie turned and narrowed her eyes. 'Different better, which is definitely a good thing. I knew this city could work its magic, like it did for me, but it took me a helluva lot longer to get to where you are. You're doing great, kid.'

Superlatives weren't Dottie's thing, so it felt like high praise I didn't deserve. All I was doing was getting through each day, but the difference was that now I was doing it with a smile on my face a lot more of the time, and after tonight, I was determined not to feel guilty about that any more.

Something in Dottie's expression made me ask, 'What brought you to New York in the first place?' But even as I spoke, whatever it was I'd caught a glimpse of disappeared.

'That's a story for another night. I need to get back to Brian and put my cold feet on his legs to warm them up. Better make sure I look okay.' My aunt took out a compact and applied some powder, followed by a fresh coat of lipstick, before spraying herself with perfume. 'I'll tell you all about that one day, but for now I'm just glad Ruby asked me if you could come and stay.'

Breathing in the familiar scent that my grandmother and great aunt both loved so much, I couldn't be annoyed about being tricked into coming to New York. I was lucky to have two such wise women in my life, and counting my blessings was something I was determined to do more of. It sounded like it had taken years for the city to help Dottie learn to let go of the past and I only had until Christmas Eve. So I'd better start making the most of every moment.

6

Exercise had always been my salvation when I felt at my lowest ebb, and regardless of my determination to start thinking more positively, I knew I needed to get out and do as much of that as I could. So, even though walking had always been more my thing, when Dannie asked me if I wanted to join him to go running the day after I went to the blues club with Dottie, it felt like an opportunity not to be missed, despite my reservations about going back to Central Park and bumping into Harry again.

We'd been jogging for about twenty minutes, when I first started trying to persuade him to stop for a drink.

'We can't stop. If you want to be able to keep eating smoked salmon and cream cheese bagels every morning, and join in with Rob's weekly cheesecake tasting, then you've got to keep moving that butt as they say over here.' Dannie was jogging on the spot as he spoke, and watching the steps racking up on his Fitbit towards his daily minimum target of 12,000. Rob had been trying out a new cheesecake recipe after every art class, and Dannie wasn't wrong when he said I'd become an enthusiastic tester, but that didn't mean I was going to let him get away with pointing it out.

'Are you calling me fat?' It was a stalling tactic, and he was on to me.

'Of course not!' Dannie grinned. 'But I'm happy to be like one of those boot camp guys who tell you how pitiful you are to make you keep going. Do you think it would help?'

'Probably not.' It was no good, I was going to have to finish the run, one way or another and preferably without Dannie having to shout 'motivational' abuse at me. Trying and failing to keep up with him, I attempted to keep the momentum going as I climbed the steps up from the Bethesda Fountain, almost running straight into Harry and Paula as I did. Dannie was already chatting, but it was going to take me a least thirty seconds to get enough breath back to speak. Wondering if I looked as unattractive as I felt, I avoided looking at Harry. Paula was as immaculate as ever, and Dannie was leaning down on the arm of her wheelchair, saying something that made her laugh. The situation made me self-conscious all over again; sweaty, out of condition and clearly lagging behind my running partner. None of that would have mattered if I hadn't been acutely aware of Harry's presence. I'd have liked to say I didn't know why it bothered me – after all, he already had a beautiful and extremely talented girlfriend, and he probably didn't even give me a second thought when I wasn't around – but I knew exactly why it mattered to me, which made things even more awkward than the unforgiving way the lycra clung to my body.

'I haven't seen you in the park for a while.' Harry gave me no choice but to look at him.

'It's been crazy in the shop.' It wasn't a lie, but I'd still managed to fit in a walk every morning before work. I'd just avoided the park. Seeing Harry stirred up unwanted feelings, and I really liked Paula, so being attracted to her partner felt wrong. It was pointless anyway and, if I was finally going to regain my ability to feel something for someone new, I didn't want to waste it on someone who lived three and a half thousand miles away.

'I've missed you.' Harry's voice was warm, and I might even have believed what he was saying, if his girlfriend hadn't been sitting six feet away from me. Maybe it was for the best. The fact that he was willing to blatantly flirt with me, when Paula could so easily overhear, ought to be enough to put me off him, but for some reason when I caught his eye, an unwelcome jolt of attraction hit me all over again. He must have felt uncomfortable when I didn't answer, though, because he changed the subject. 'Have you heard about the wall art under the Greywacke Arch? Paula and I were just going to check it out. Why don't you guys come, too; maybe we could all grab a coffee afterwards?'

'Aren't you supposed to be working?' There was an accusatory tone to my voice, as if I'd suddenly turned into his boss, but it was a form of defence. I didn't want to allow myself to become as friendly towards Harry as he was being towards me, not if I was going to keep these stupid unwanted feelings in check.

'No, I'm all done for the day.' Harry smiled, turning towards Paula and Dannie. 'So, what do you think? Shall we go and check it out?'

'Sounds great!' Dannie answered for both of us. 'Is it something the park commissioned?' He didn't look at all disappointed to finish our run.

'Apparently not and everyone seems to think it's a Parsy.' Paula widened her eyes as she spoke, and I tried to work out what that meant. There were still quite a few Americanisms I was struggling to get to grips with and there was some truth in us being separated by a common language. I had no idea what a Parsy was, but Dannie hadn't missed my blank look.

'A Parsy is a bit like a Banksy, only less political. They've been appearing in places all over Manhattan for the last couple of years, and no one knows who's doing them. It'll be really exciting if it is one. There's been a bit of copycat stuff, but there's a Twitter account where he confirms whether it's his or not. Although I think you can tell if it's the real deal, he's brilliant.'

'Or she,' Harry said, as we quickened our pace to keep up with Paula. 'No one knows and I think that's part of what's built the artist's reputation.'

There was a crowd gathered by the arch, but Paula was obviously an old hand at clearing a path, and it wasn't long before we got to the front. Dannie had been right when he'd said that Parsy had a similar style to Banksy, but the image was softer and more colourful. It had a row of green benches, like the ones in the park, with replicas of some of the plaques I'd seen on my first day there, and couples of all ages and genders sitting on either side of the plaques. Above the picture were the words: *'Love stories. Every one.'*

'How did someone manage to do all this without anyone seeing?' The words caught in my throat. I didn't profess to know anything about art, but it was truly breath-taking. Parsy had captured exactly what I'd thought when I was reading the bench plaques. Every one of them was like a mini love story, or a love letter to someone lost. Whoever the artist was, they clearly thought so too.

'It's amazing what he's done on the side of buildings without being spotted. Apparently, that wall, where he painted the forest scene, is going to be auctioned off. I read that they're expecting it to make at least a million dollars.' Dannie let out a long breath. 'What I don't understand is how Parsy gets his hands on any of that money. If he's anonymous, how does he get paid?'

'He doesn't.' Paula turned her wheelchair around. 'I don't think it's about that. It's a way of expressing something that money can't buy and sharing that with an audience, in a way they can connect with.'

'See, that's why you're a doctor and I sell cheesecake.' Dannie laughed. 'Talking of which, I better get back and give Rob a hand, or our love story might be over. Are you coming, Lib?'

I hesitated, casting a quick glance at Harry. He looked back at me, his eyes twinkling, and I felt that familiar jolt somewhere inside me. 'Actually, I think I'll go for that coffee with Paula and Harry.' Maybe I was a secret masochist. Spending time with Harry and his girlfriend might prove torturous, but I was weirdly fascinated by the dynamics of their relationship and I'd never met a less possessive couple. That must be what complete confidence did for you. I'd never had that, only a boyfriend who'd headed for the hills when the going got tough and I couldn't be the always-up-for-fun girlfriend any more. If I ever did have another relationship, I wanted it to be with someone who was there for all of it, no matter how hard, and it looked like Harry and Paula might already have found that.

'Okay, you can have coffee elsewhere, but no bagels or cheese-cake in another shop. As far as Rob's concerned, that would count as adultery.' Dannie turned and set off along the path as I followed Harry and Paula from under the arch in a different direction, and at a much slower pace. A jogger was heading towards us at pace, and I couldn't help but take him in. He was a tall man, with the sort of muscle tone that I thought only existed on the air-brushed covers of fitness magazines. It was a good job Dannie had already left, or he'd have had serious ab envy – I was sure I could make them out, even through his T-shirt. He wasn't my type: too high maintenance. But I wasn't sure I even had a type any more. Then, as Harry suddenly stopped, and I accidentally brushed against him, I discovered I did have a type after all. The unfortunate part was that my type was in a relationship.

'DeShawn!' Harry called out to the super-toned runner, and the guy slowed down as he approached us.

'Hey, great to see you.' DeShawn addressed them both, but he didn't take his eyes off Paula.

'This is Libby, she was admiring your kaleidoscope picture at the Community Center.' Harry introduced me, and DeShawn smiled and held out his hand.

'Nice to meet you, Libby. DeShawn Parshall.'

'Nice to meet you too, DeShawn.'

'So' – he was looking at Paula again – 'have you thought any more about my invitation? To the exhibition, I mean? After all, I owe it all to you, my fantastic art tutor.'

'DeShawn's got his first exhibition.' Paula turned to look at me, her cheeks flushed. 'Although, I don't know why he's giving me any credit. He was already a fantastic artist when he first walked into my classes. I've never been able to work out why he kept coming.'

'I can think of one good reason.' DeShawn gave her an intense look and I snuck a glance at Harry. He was smiling. This was getting seriously weird. There was one thing being confident enough not to mind your partner indulging in a bit of flirting with someone else, but there was an electricity between DeShawn and Paula to make even me want to blush. Suddenly a horrible thought struck me. Maybe they were swingers. To each their own and all that, but it would definitely shatter my illusion of them as the perfect couple.

'Look I've got to go, but let me know about the exhibition, okay? It won't be the same without you.' DeShawn was already barely visible in the distance, by the time anyone spoke again.

'So, come on, Paula. Are you finally going to admit I was right about DeShawn wanting to share more than his artwork with you?' Harry was making a joke about his girlfriend and another man, and I was starting to wish I'd jogged all the way back to Seventh Avenue with Dannie.

'Okay, okay, you're right as usual!' Paula was always so polished and professional, but she'd turned into a giggly schoolgirl in front of my eyes. 'The question is, what shall I do about it?'

'It's pretty obvious you like him, too. So, go to the exhibition and see where it leads.'

This was definitely too much for me now. I couldn't keep standing there, listening, while Harry all but set his girlfriend up with DeShawn. It was making me feel a bit sick, and the only upside was that Harry had finally dropped down in my estimation. In fact, I'd gone right off him.

'I'm sorry, I should probably leave you two to it... I'm not sure how open relationships work, but it seems like you've got a lot to talk about, and the last thing you need is me hanging around.' I'd worried that my imagination had been running away with me, when it had felt like Harry was flirting. Now I was more worried I might be right. I really enjoyed spending time with my new friends, but I didn't want things to get awkward between us.

'Open relationships?' Harry put a hand on my arm to stop me bolting. I might not have been able to run as fast as DeShawn or even Dannie, but I'd never wanted to disappear into the distance more in my life. 'Wait a minute, you don't think Paula and I are together, do you?'

'Oh my God, you did, didn't you?' Paula pulled a face. 'Sorry, but gross. He's like my little brother.'

'But you kissed, at the Community Center, and I...' I wasn't even sure how to finish that sentence, because now I couldn't pinpoint exactly when, or even why I'd decided they were a couple.

'Yes, I kissed her, *on the cheek*. I know you Brits have got a reputation for being a bit repressed, but even you guys do that, don't you?' Harry was openly laughing now and I felt my face flush with embarrassment.

'We went to art college together, and we've been close friends ever since. We even shared an apartment once.' Paula pulled another face. 'But let's just say you weren't the only one to mistake him for my boyfriend, and at one stage back then it started to seriously affect my love life.'

'Now you're doing that for yourself.' Harry gave her a level look, and she bit her lip. I felt like I was intruding again, but for completely different reasons this time.

'It's just since I've been in this thing.' Paula thumped the armrest of her wheelchair. 'I seem to have lost my confidence about dating.'

'And DeShawn's the perfect person to help you get that back.' Harry put a hand on her shoulder. 'He knows how lucky he'd be to have you in his life, and it's about time you realised that too.'

'Stop being nice to me, or I'm going to have to run over your foot.' Paula kept her eyes on the path in front of her. I wouldn't have guessed in a million years that she had a crisis of confidence about anything. It just proved how good people were at hiding things and I'd had a lot of practice of doing just that.

'I'll stop being nice to you, if you promise to go out with DeShawn.' Harry sped up so that he passed her wheelchair and could stand in front of it, blocking her path.

'Okay, okay, if it'll make you happy, I'll do it.' The smile that had spread over Paula's face made it clear Harry wasn't the only one who was happy about the prospect of her going on a date with DeShawn.

'Now we've sorted that, shall we go and get some coffee?' Harry turned to me and I nodded, still a little sheepish from my awkward blunder before. It was obvious that he really cared about Paula and that he was willing to risk her being annoyed with him for pushing her into a date with DeShawn, even if the gamble had paid off. There was just one problem with all of that: instead of going off him, I liked him more than ever. And quite frankly, it terrified me.

7

On the morning of Thanksgiving, I woke up thinking about my parents. Dannie and Rob would be cooking dinner and I'd been invited to join them and my other new friends to experience the parade. But as I opened my eyes, the ache of missing Mum and Dad was suddenly overwhelming.

I picked up the phone, scrolling down to Dannie's number. I was going to have to tell them I wanted to cancel, but then something stopped me. Light was already streaming in through the window, and it was as if my legs had a mind of their own as I stood up and crossed the room. Looking down at the street below, there was a couple, probably in their early thirties, both wearing hats shaped like turkeys and holding the hands of a little girl who was beaming with excitement. Without warning, it was like I'd been taken back more than twenty years, to the day my parents had taken me to a pantomime, when I must have been about eight or nine. Mum had insisted on us all wearing matching elf hats. We'd ended up having to rush to make the performance, after struggling to get parked, and the sight of the oversized ears on Dad's hat swinging to and fro as he ran, had made me laugh so much I'd had to stop running. Then my parents had stopped too and the laughter had been contagious. I could still picture the look on Mum's face as she tried and failed to find a way of tucking the fake ears up inside Dad's hat.

She'd always had this knack of squeezing every possible bit of fun from a situation, which had helped create the memories that had meant so much since I'd lost them. If Mum had been given the chance to experience Thanksgiving, we'd all have been wearing crazy headgear like the family who'd just rushed by on the street below my window, before disappearing into Dannie and Rob's deli. And any thought I'd had of cancelling was forgotten. I wanted to watch the parade – not just for myself, but because everything I did in New York made me feel somehow closer to my parents, despite them never making it here. Whatever the reason, I couldn't help smiling as I looked across at the elf's hat lying on top of my coat, on the chair beside the bed. I'd forgotten all about that trip to the panto when Maddison had offered to lend me a hat I could wear to the parade, but now it had all coming flooding back. I needed to speak to someone who understood that I could miss my parents like crazy, but still want to experience everything New York had to offer because of them. It was only breakfast time in Manhattan, but it was lunchtime back home and Nan was the only person I wanted to talk to.

'I think you're picking up a bit of an accent already, Lib!' She answered the phone after only a couple of rings, sounding almost as pleased to speak to me as I was to hear her voice.

'Well, *you* sound exactly the same. I miss you.' I really did. Even though I was having a far better time in New York than I'd ever imagined I would. She'd been right to pack me off to help Aunt Dottie, but then she was always right. Which was exactly why I needed to speak to her.

'We miss you too, darling, but I can't believe you've been

there almost a month already.' There were glasses clinking and the sound of laughter in the background; it certainly seemed like they were managing to keep the micro-pub running without me. No doubt the regulars were visiting even more often, to make up for the fact they'd be missing some visits when my grandparents went on their cruise. 'Although Dottie tells me you've got a pretty good social life going on, and that she hardly gets to see you.'

'I've met some lovely people and Aunt Dottie's pretty busy with her own life, too.' I had a strong suspicion that her hip had already been more or less healed by the time I'd arrived. Especially as Dottie had already all but confessed that it was a ruse they'd cooked up between the two of them for my benefit. It didn't matter any more, because I was glad they had.

'So, you're having a good time?'

'I am.'

'And you're happy?'

'Yes...'

'But?'

'But it's weird. Somehow, I feel closer to Mum and Dad here than I did at home. How can that possibly be the case when Canterbury is where I grew up and every street seems to have some memory of them?'

'Maybe it's because it's where you lost them too.' As soon as Nan had said the words, I knew she was right. 'When you're at home, every place that reminds you of them has a gaping hole it in now they're not here. You haven't got those memories in New York, so you can think about how much they would have loved it instead. The three of you were so close, it must be quite easy for you to picture how they would have reacted to the things you're seeing. Rather than being here and seeing the empty spaces where they used to be, you've taken them with you.'

'That's exactly it.' My breath caught in my throat. 'Is that why you're going on the cruise?'

'We always said we'd do it with your mum and dad after we finally retired from this place, but we left it too late.' Nan let out a shuddering sigh. 'Going away means I won't have to look up every time the door opens and expect to see them coming through it. I'm hoping they'll come with me on the cruise, like they've been with you. But even if they're not, I know it'll be different to the emptiness there is without them here.'

'I wish you'd told me how you felt.' I'd have done anything to be able to wrap my arms around her. But even as I said the words, I understood why Nan had kept it to herself. She hadn't wanted to give in to her grief, because she'd been too busy protecting me.

'I had your granddad to talk to about it; he understood exactly what it was like for me to lose a child, because he'd lost her too. You didn't have anyone who understood what you were going through and I wasn't about to add to that. But hearing you now, it's like music to my ears. I was starting to think you might never talk about being happy again.' Nan let out another long breath. 'Your mum and dad would have desperately wanted you to be happy too. You were the most important thing in the world to them.'

'I know.' It had taken me a while, but I was finally starting to allow myself to enjoy life again and I knew they'd have been relieved if they were still around to see it.

'And if you decide you want to stay on for bit longer, your granddad and I can manage fine here.'

'Don't worry, I'll be back before you're home for New Year, just like I said I would.' I hadn't told my grandparents that I was planning on coming home on Christmas Eve, because I knew they'd worry about me being on my own. When I'd agreed to go to New York, it had felt like the only way I could do it. I couldn't spend Christmas in the city my mother had loved from afar. There'd be too many memories of all the festive movies set here, which we'd watched together in the run up to Christmas every year. She'd talk about how much she wanted to visit and how amazing it would be to spend the holidays here. I couldn't do that without her, but I knew it would have broken Nan's heart if I told her. Yet, as the words came out of my mouth, I couldn't help but feel differently about returning to the UK. I tried to focus on the excitement of seeing my grandparents again and not picture Harry's face, which seemed to flit into my mind every chance it got, especially now I knew he was single. I shook myself. I wasn't in the right place for a relationship, and thankfully he seemed to sense that too. The timing was wrong, and despite how much more positive I was feeling, I wasn't sure when it would ever be right again.

* * *

'So, your aunt's in Vegas for Thanksgiving?' Rob took a pecan pie out of the oven as he spoke, and Dannie looked at his watch yet again.

I nodded. 'She did ask me if I wanted to go with her and Brian.' I gave a little involuntary shudder. 'But one of the things she was most excited about was the hot tub in the condo they've rented. And the sight of her and Brian, in the bubbles, isn't something I was sure I'd be able to give thanks for.'

'That's pretty awesome, though. I hope I've got a sex life like that by the time I'm their age.' Rob folded out a cardboard box ready for when the pecan pie had finished cooling on the rack.

'Don't get me wrong, I love the fact she's recovered so well from her operation, and that she's having so much *fun*. But I don't think they really wanted me there, any more than I wanted to be there.'

'It's a good job you've got such great company for the day then.' Dannie walked over and gave me a hug. He might have been fishing for a compliment, but it was true. I was lucky. Within weeks, I'd found a circle of friends in New York that I hadn't had since my university days. But we weren't friends because we had a school or a job in common, and the connection I felt to them was different from anything I'd experienced before. I hadn't had as much time to catch up with old friends once I'd started work in London, and it turned out that most of the friends I'd made through work were only there for the good times, like Ryan. Admittedly, one or two of them had tried to support me after my parents died and some of my old friends had reached out too, but I'd pushed them away because I didn't feel like the person they used to know any more. Maybe that's why I appreciated what I'd found in Manhattan; it was easy to remember that nothing was forever, and to make the most of the time I had with them. And they couldn't compare the person I was now with the old version of me either.

'It's great getting to share the holiday with all of you and I'm really looking forward to experiencing my first Thanksgiving.' I glanced at the bags on the table, where Rob had already packed up enough food to feed a family for at least a week. We were going to Central Park, to meet up with Harry and the others and watch Macy's Thanksgiving Parade as it passed along the Upper West Side. Then we were going back to the Community Center for a Thanksgiving dinner.

'Right Rob, are you nearly done?' Dannie's tone wasn't one that could be ignored. 'Because if I miss the beginning of the parade, you'll be wearing that pecan pie as a hat.'

'That would be a waste of a great pie, but luckily I'm ready to go. We can swing by here afterwards and pick everything up to go to the Community Center.' Rob took hold of Dannie's hand and the three of us headed out on to the street. I was about to experience my first ever Thanksgiving, and I already felt as though I had more to be thankful for than I'd had in a very long time.

* * *

It seemed as if half of America had turned out on the streets of New York to watch the parade. A lot of the crowds were heading towards Sixth Avenue, but there were plenty of people going in the same direction as us, and I wondered if we'd even manage to meet up with the others.

As it was, they were easy to find. Madison had obviously decided to tie in with the theme of the hat she'd leant me and was dressed as an elf, but not with oversized ears or trousers that stopped at the knee. She was wearing shorts, with less material than my hat, and stripy red and white tights that made her legs look like they went all the way to her chin. I had to admit she looked stunning, even if it did make me feel ancient. Paula, Abbie and Karly were there, too. Even the pugs had put in an appearance, although they looked as though they'd rather be back snoring on their sofa in the Community Center.

When Harry turned up with flasks of hot chocolate he'd made for everyone, I moved to stand next to him. He was wearing a grey trench coat and a ribbed navy-blue sweater, and I found myself thinking he could warm me up far more quickly than the hot chocolate. A heat crept up my neck at the thought, but it was also refreshing to feel this way about someone again. It was all part of the progress I'd made in New York, and just another reason to be thankful, because it meant that the part of me I'd assumed was dead might not be gone forever after all. Nothing was going to happen with Harry, but the idea that I might want it to one day, with someone else, was something to hold on to.

I'd seen snippets of the parade in films, but it was even more of a spectacle than I imagined. Huge balloons rose above the floats, and I watched everything from Charlie Brown to Thomas the Tank Engine, and a huge Thanksgiving turkey, float by. The crowds surged forward as the float carrying Santa Claus drew level with us, and the expression on the face of a little boy sitting on his dad's shoulders, to the left of me, made me smile. If there was such a thing as magic, it could be captured by the look in his eyes and another memory flashed into my mind. Dad had dressed up as Santa for my primary school's Christmas fayre every December, and I hadn't realised until years later that it had been him. The magic had been enough for me to overlook the fact that Santa wore exactly the same signet ring on his little finger as my dad, with a lion's head on a black background, that his own father had given him. Watching that little boy was like recapturing a part my childhood for a few minutes and it was happening more and more. Every time it did I was hit by that same feeling again – the sense that my parents were right there with me. I hadn't allowed myself to recall any of those things the first Christmas they were gone. But there were hundreds of happy memories – gifts just waiting to be opened – and being in New York was finally allowing me to relive the good times one by one.

'What did you think of the parade?' Harry and I fell into step with one another as we walked back towards the Community Center. Abbie and Madison had offered to go to the deli with Dannie and Rob, to pick up the food, and Karly had gone on ahead to open up. Paula was meeting with DeShawn, who was a volunteer on one of the floats, and he was going to be joining us for dinner. It looked like Harry's matchmaking was paying off.

'It was even better than I thought it would be. The crowds were crazy, but I wouldn't have missed it for the world.'

'I know what you mean about the crowds. I love this city, but I think I love it best when it's early in the morning, on a cold day, and I seem to have most of the park to myself.'

'I'd be the same.' Our hands were so close, and the sidewalks were still so crowded, that every few steps our fingers would brush against each other. I didn't attempt to move farther away. There were too many people jostling us anyway. But even if the sidewalk had been empty, I wouldn't have wanted to move. 'I've fallen in love with everything about this city, but the park is my favourite place. I'm with Parsy – that picture under the arch summed it up for me. I could spend a week just reading the plaques on the benches.'

'I spend a lot of my lunch hours that way. It gives me inspiration.'

'Inspiration?' I knew Harry could draw, because I'd seen his work at our art classes, and he'd told me a bit more about going to college with Paula. They'd been through art school together, and then she'd gone on to train as a psychotherapist. Although, from what he'd said, I didn't think he did much outside the art classes any more. But, from the beginning, I suppose we'd always spoken more about me than him and it was time to put that right.

'Yeah, I'm writing a book. Actually, it's my third, and I've already got two out with agents and publishers under considera-tion. But I've probably got more chance of winning the Powerball than actually getting a publisher.'

If Harry thought he was more likely to win the lottery than get published, he clearly wasn't remotely confident about finding an audience for his books, which made me suspect he'd either written about an obscure artist or produced an A-Z of the insects native to Central Park. There was only one way to find out. 'What kind of books do you write?'

'They're kids' books. I illustrate them myself, too.' Harry laughed. 'Although I'm not sure if that will count in my favour, or go against me. There's one about a magic wishing bench, and I get almost all of my ideas while I'm in the park.' He looked down at the sidewalk, as if he wished he hadn't mentioned it.

'That sounds great. I'd love to read it one day.' And I meant it. Something in the way Harry spoke about his writing and illustrating gave me the feeling he had a far better chance of finding a publisher than he thought.

'We've all got to have a dream, I suppose, but I'm lucky. Even if it never gets better than working in the park, I'll be happy.'

I turned to look at him then. 'Do you know what my dream would be?' I asked quietly. He shook his head. I hadn't told anyone about wanting to do this, not even Nan, but ever since the first day in the park, I hadn't been able to stop thinking about it. 'I wish I could dedicate one of the benches in the park to my parents. But I looked it up, and it costs ten thousand dollars. I really would have to win the lottery to stretch to that.'

'I know, it's crazy, isn't it?'

'If you see me scratching their names on one of the benches with a screwdriver, or writing the message on with a marker pen, just promise me you'll turn a blind eye.'

'Don't worry, I'd just be looking at you, anyway, not what you were doing.' Harry caught my eye for a moment and my stomach did that weird fluttering thing it had a habit of doing every time he was around, before he looked down at the ground again. We suddenly seemed in danger of stepping over a line that both of us had been backing away from since the first day we met.

'So, how come you aren't spending Thanksgiving with your family?' Turning the conversation back around to him wasn't just a way of changing the subject. Harry knew far more about me than I'd ever intended him to, but I knew next to nothing about him and the more I found out the more he intrigued me. In the last ten minutes, I'd already discovered he had a secret life as an author and illustrator. I wanted to know about his background too and to hear what his childhood had been like. I wanted to learn everything there was to know about Harry and there was no point even trying to pretend I felt that to the same extent about the rest of our group of friends.

'My sister lives in San Francisco, and she's got two kids, so my parents spend all the holidays with them. I get invited, of course, and I'll probably fly down for Christmas, but me and Paula have hung out together at Thanksgiving since we were at college. Besides, why would you want to be anywhere but New York for all of this?'

'I think my first Thanksgiving is going to spoil me for any others I might experience in the future.'

'Do you ever think about staying? In New York, I mean?' He stopped, and for a split second I wanted to admit that it was something I'd begun to imagine, but my life was in Canterbury. My grandparents might finally be willing to take a holiday, but they'd go back to the pub after their break and they'd need me to be there too. Even if they insisted they could run the pub without me, they weren't getting any younger and, before too long, they might need someone to start looking after them. They'd already lost their only daughter, there was no way I could abandon them too. Except part of me was terrified that, when I went home, all the good memories of my parents would disappear again and the only thing I'd be able to see would be those empty spaces Nan had talked about. But looking up at Harry again, I knew it wasn't just the fear of that making me want to stay. I wanted more time with him. It was ridiculous and I hardly even knew him, but right then the idea of being in New York with Harry felt more like home than anything else.

'It's great here, and I've felt more at ease, almost from the second my cab arrived on Seventh Avenue, than I ever thought I could.' He'd probably think I was crazy when I told him why I thought that was, but I didn't seem to be able to stop myself from saying it. 'Maybe's it's because I've seen New York so often in films, and because I came here on a couple of business trips a few years ago, but even when I go to places I've never been before, it feels like I know them. I never felt this connected to the place on my previous trips, but this time it's like coming home.'

'I felt that connection when I moved here for college, and I knew I could never leave. I might not have been born a New Yorker, but it has a way of getting under your skin. At least for some of us.'

'This is probably going to sound insane.' I figured I might as well tell him the rest, now that I'd started, but even if I'd tried to stop I don't think I'd have been able to. 'The thing is, I've felt the same about you, too, since that first time we spoke up at the castle. It was like I'd met you before, and I kept wondering if you just really looked like someone on TV, or if I'd met you on one of my previous trips.'

'I'd have remembered you, if I'd ever met you before.' His voice was low and my pulse seemed to be thudding in my ears. It was a good job we were only a hundred feet or so from the Community Center, because if we'd had more time alone together, I might have told him how I really felt, and the realisation of what I really felt was terrifying.

'I guess some people just connect more easily.' I attempted a casual shrug, keeping my tone light. 'In your job, you've probably just developed the knack of making people feel comfortable talking to you.'

For a moment Harry didn't speak and then he stopped again as we reached the door of the Community Center. 'I felt it too – that connection.'

Holding my breath, I knew if I made the wrong move I'd ruin

everything. I couldn't risk the fragile happiness I'd found here, that I desperately wanted to hold on to until I boarded my plane home at JFK. Every nerve ending in my body was urging me to reach out and touch him, but the thought of what that might lead to was too overwhelming. His hand was barely an inch away from mine, but I'd never needed to listen to my head over my heart more than I needed to right then. If that meant lying to Harry, it was just something I needed to do.

'I'm glad, because I felt it with all of you – Dannie, Rob, Paula, even Madison.' I was desperately trying to backtrack and make it sound like the connection I'd described having with Harry was nothing special. I had no idea if he was convinced, but if I could just make it inside with the others before my face gave me away, it might be enough. 'We'd better not keep them waiting; I don't think Rob's pecan pie is going to last long.'

'It's Paula's favourite, so you're probably right.' The tension left Harry's face, like a man who'd realised he'd had a narrow escape, and I couldn't stop my shoulders from slumping. It was madness when his reaction to my words was what I'd wanted, to pass the connection between us off as nothing, but I hadn't expected him to so readily accept it. Suddenly not even the thought of Rob's pecan pie could cheer me up.

* * *

'I think I might be broken.' Dannie massaged his stomach as he pushed his plate away from him, and I knew exactly how he felt. The food had been incredible. Rob and Karly had done an amazing job pulling the Thanksgiving dinner together in the small kitchen of the Community Center and the even tinier one in Karly's apartment at the back of the building. Their cooking skills must have run in the family, because Karly had taken care of the turkey, stuffing and yams, with her pugs fixated on her every move when they was being served. It was a miracle she didn't trip over them when she was walking backwards and forwards to the table.

Abbie had contributed a huge bowl of macaroni and cheese, and Madison had made corn bread. Paula and Harry had taken care of the drinks. I felt guilty for not contributing to the party, but they'd all insisted that they wanted to show me a proper Thanksgiving, so I wasn't allowed to bring anything. After the main course, I hadn't been sure I could eat any dessert, but, somehow, I'd managed not only a slice of pecan pie, but a spiced apple and pumpkin muffin too.

The four pugs were stretched out snoring after the meal was over, probably because too many slices of turkey had been dropped under the table for them, and it was tempting to join them. Abbie was keen to show off her acting talents, though, and she was trying to rally us into a game of twenty questions once we'd cleared up. But the general consensus was that watching an American football game, on the big TV in the Community Center crèche, was the best way to recover from all that overindulgence. It was one of the few things that still felt like it belonged to an alien culture. American football. I just didn't get it, and I couldn't seem to make head nor tail of what was going on, probably because I didn't want to. So when DeShawn and Paula suggested going out for a walk, and asked if anyone else wanted to join them, I didn't hesitate. I felt a bit guilty – I was sure they wanted to be on their own really, but I had no intention of trailing around with them for long. I just wanted a reason to get out for a bit, to clear my head. It was great being surrounded by everyone, and they'd all made me feel so welcome, but I needed some time on my own to decompress and process this day meant for sharing with loved ones. When I'd looked at some of the pictures from the parade, my first instinct had been to text Mum and send them to her. I'd got a great shot of the Paddington Bear float and he'd been one of her favourites, but she'd never get to see the picture. It still blindsided me how things like that could hit me so hard, as if the air had been knocked out of my lungs. But I was getting better at coping with it, especially lately, and time outside walking always helped.

'I'll come with you.' Harry was up on his feet before I had a chance to try and put him off. I'd been counting on some time alone to process my feelings for him too, because they'd blind-sided me in a very different way. My eyes had kept sliding in his direction all through dinner, and the last time I could remember feeling like that had been when I was about fourteen and I'd convinced myself I was in love with our next-door neighbour's son, Tom. It was a proper schoolgirl crush, with his name scrawled on almost every page of the journal I used to keep back then. I defi-nitely hadn't expected to feel like that at this age, and the last thing I needed was my newfound crush walking by my side, reminding me of all the reasons why he'd be more than worthy of filling the pages of my journal, if I still kept one.

'We could go for a drink somewhere if you want?' The words came out of Paula's mouth as we got outside, but her eyes said something else.

'Not for me, thanks. I fancy a walk up to the Empire State Building. I love seeing it lit up at night.' I glanced at Harry as I spoke, and he raised a questioning eyebrow. For some reason I nodded. There was no denying that part of me wanted his company, even though I knew I was taking a risk.

We left Paula and DeShawn to their own nighttime stroll, and walked in silence towards the Empire State Building. Weirdly, it didn't feel awkward. When I'd first started working in the shop, with Madison and Betty, the three of us had talked about anything and everything, just to avoid that awkward silence that could arise when you were getting to know someone. But I could be with

Harry and say nothing, and he seemed to instinctively understand when that was what I needed to do. If I'd written a list of pros and cons about him, the way my friends and I used to do about boys when we were teenagers, the only thing on the cons side would be that he lived a six-hour plane ride away from where the rest of my life was.

'I love this building.' I was the first to speak in the end, and I smiled at the memory that always came back to me when I saw the building that was lit up in front of us. 'The first time I was in New York, I didn't have a lot of time for sight-seeing, but the one place I was determined to see was the Empire State Building. I followed the Google maps app on my phone, and I was on Thirty-Fourth Street but it was such a misty day that I couldn't see it at all. So I stopped and spoke to a police officer on the corner of Fifth Avenue, and asked him where it was. He laughed so hard that he could hardly point out that I was standing right in front of it.' The top of the building had been shrouded in mist and, standing right next to it, without being able to see the iconic pinnacle from where the *King Kong* movie had created such an iconic image, it looked like the bottom of any other skyscraper. It had given the police officer a good laugh at the time, and it seemed to be having the same effect on Harry.

'Not big enough for you to spot then?'

I nudged him in the ribs and he caught hold of me and spun me round to face him. I should have stopped him when he kissed me, but I didn't want to. The lid had flipped off the box that was never supposed to be opened in an instant, and it turned out I had no intention of slamming it shut again. Being rational about our situation and what the future held was proving much more diffi-cult when it came to Harry.

'I've been wanting to do that since the first day I met you, and you admitted that *The Smurfs* was your favourite movie.' He laughed softly, his breath warm against my cheek.

'I did *not* say it was my favourite!'

'And there I was thinking I'd met my soul mate.' I couldn't tell if he was still joking, but he had to be. We'd known each other for less than a month, and he knew as well as I did that I was almost halfway through my stay already. For all I knew, he did this all the time, meeting girls whose time in New York was limited from the start. Like a waiter in a holiday resort, finding his 'soul mate' each time someone new got off the tour bus, hours after the 'soul mate' before her caught the plane home again.

'Sorry to be the bearer of bad news, but I'm sure your Smurf loving soul mate is out there somewhere.' I laughed, but something inside me twisted at the idea of Harry finding his person and it not being me, which was insane given that I'd barely known him for a month. Still, I'd be long gone by then and, if I kept in contact with him, I'd eventually hear about it on Instagram or something. Hopefully my feelings for Harry would be long gone by then too. Although I had to admit that the kiss hadn't helped on that front. Ideally it would have been awful, but it had been sweet and gentle at first, building to a promise of more to come and I hadn't wanted it to stop, despite the fact that public displays of affection were definitely not my thing. I'd seen *Sleepless in Seattle* far too many times, that was all. It was the Empire State Building's fault, for helping put the idea of romance back into my head when I'd been so determined to push it out.

'Okay so we might not be soul mates and your membership to the Smurf fan club might be revoked forever, but will you at least let me show you what Christmas in New York has to offer?' Harry waited for me to answer, and, somehow, I found myself nodding. I had no idea what was going on with me. I had to back off – I *needed* to back off for self-preservation – but something kept stopping me.

It was like I'd picked up the wrong script for a Broadway play, and ended up in a scene from one of Abbie's alternative theatre shows instead. I knew what I was supposed to say, but the words didn't fit the scene, and I ended up ad-libbing, saying yes, when I should be saying no. I had no idea how it was going to end, I just knew that it was.

'I'd like that.' I closed my eyes as he kissed me again, letting myself pretend for a minute that this was my life and that if my feelings for Harry turned out not to just be a schoolgirl crush, we had the option of seeing where it went. I wanted to take up his offer of seeing New York through his eyes, for me and my parents, even though I knew there was every chance of it hurting like hell when I had to say goodbye. I'd promised not to let myself risk that kind of hurt, but as I leant into him, I didn't care. If losing my parents had taught me anything, it should have been that the biggest regrets were for the things you never got to experience. Whatever happened, I knew for sure I'd regret not spending the next four weeks with Harry. So, I'd just have to deal with the consequences when it was over.

8

———

A week after Thanksgiving, New York had gone into full Christmas mode, and December had arrived with the first flurry of snow. I'd been on a couple of low-key dates with Harry: the first was at an improv comedy night that Abbie had hosted at the Community Center, and I'd invited Dannie and Rob along to our second date, at a restaurant in China Town. Despite taking the decision to spend more time with him, in the knowledge that I'd regret it if I didn't, I was still desperately trying to stop myself from falling for Harry in the way I suspected I could. But I couldn't keep using other people to protect me from that. I just had to keep reminding myself that, in four weeks' time, New York would just be a distant memory, and there was every chance that Harry would be introducing himself to someone else at Belvedere Castle. The trouble was, I envied that someone already.

It wasn't just the prospect of leaving Harry and the rest of my friends that made it feel as though the days were whizzing by far too quickly. I'd come to love working in the shop more than I'd ever have dreamed possible and I was beginning to wonder how I'd ever settle back into the slow pace of life at the micro-pub. We were run off our feet during opening hours, and today was no exception. I didn't have time to unpack the latest delivery until after I'd finally served the last customers of the day – a Dutch family, who were buying decorations for various family members, and had spent twice as many dollars in an hour than I'd earned since I'd been in New York. I'd sent Betty and Madison home and, once I opened the box, I was glad I had.

It was a delivery of snow globes, and I wasn't sure whether to expect tacky plastic Statues of Liberty encased in the glass, or something else entirely. Most of the decorations in Candy Cane Lane were high end, but my great aunt had long since cottoned on to the need to cater for all sectors of the market, and so there were *those* kinds of decorations too. But the snow globes were definitely not tacky. Each one contained a beautiful, hand-sculpted Christmas tree, and the detail on the decorations was exquisite. Some of the trees were very traditional and hung with red, green and gold decorations, and others looked like they'd been dressed with homemade decorations, with strings of popcorn and ginger-bread men. They made me want to climb inside the globes, especially the one that was decorated to celebrate family life. It had a tiny pair of ballet shoes hanging from one branch, mittens, and snowmen that looked as though they'd been made from cotton wool balls. It reminded me of the tree we'd had at home when I was a child. Mum had hung whatever decorations I'd made at school in pride of place, no matter how awful they were. I remembered one: a polystyrene cup, with a few bits of glitter stuck to the side, and a fluffy green pipe cleaner rammed through the middle with a bell on the end, that would never ring against the side of the cup. Anyone would have thought it had been made by Tiffany, the way she looked at it. Maybe it was because I'd ended up being a miracle only child – despite being a surprise early on in my parents' relationship. They'd had tests to see why they couldn't have more children, and they'd been told that they should never have been able to conceive at all. Mum had told me later that they'd never even thought about going through treatment to have another child, and they'd just counted their blessings every day that they had me. It was another of those unexplained feelings, but it felt as if the snow globe had captured my childhood and that, if I could just get inside it, I could go back. I shook myself as I set the last of the snow globes on the shelf.

Unpacking the delivery had made me cry, but they weren't tears of sadness. I knew if I'd seen that snow globe back in a shop in Canterbury, I'd have run out into the street, tears streaming down my face, only able to think about what I'd lost. But something had irrevocably shifted in me since I'd come to New York. I thought about the good times with my parents now far more often than I thought about their deaths. Every time I met up with Harry, it seemed to lead to me telling him another story about them. When he'd mentioned wanting to take me to China Town, we'd laughed together when I told him about the time my parents had gone to China Town in London, for their anniversary. Dad had struggled to chew something in one of the dishes he'd ordered, only to swallow it whole to avoid the embarrassment of spitting it out. When one of the waiters had started looking under the tables for something he'd lost, Dad had asked what was wrong. It turned out that the rubber thumb he used to count the notes when he was tilling up had gone missing. When Harry had asked if Dad had been worried that he'd swallowed it, I'd told him that my father's only reaction had been relief that he hadn't accidentally ordered the sheep's penis soup that was a delicacy on the restaurant's menu. It had been a running joke between my parents afterwards, that whenever Dad asked what was for dinner, my mother would say sheep's penis soup. Telling the story, I could picture them so clearly – Dad rolling his eyes and saying 'not again, I had that last night' – and it felt like Harry was getting to know my parents too, and I loved that feeling.

One of the things I'd thought about a lot after they'd died and Ryan had decided we were finished, was that if I did eventually meet someone, my parents would never know him. Worse still, he'd never know them. But talking to Harry had made me realise I had the power to fix that last part and to bring my parents back to life, a little at a time, until the person I ended up with could picture them almost as clearly as I could. It was another reason I'd always be grateful that Nan and Aunt Dottie had tricked me into coming to New York and that I'd met Harry, someone who'd given me the space to realise that talking about my parents could really help me to heal. It was part of the reason why I decided to keep one snow globe back. And I was just taking the money from my bag, to put in the till, when Aunt Dottie arrived.

'Surely things aren't that bad, that you're having to top up the till?' Her voice made me jump. She was definitely getting better – I hadn't even heard her unlock the door, let alone come in, and her foldable walking stick was still hanging from her wrist, in its folded-up state.

'I was just putting the money in the till for one of these snow globes.' I'd have been mortified if Aunt Dottie thought I was taking something from her.

'Why on earth are you doing that?' Her hair was back to its purple best, and she had a shiny purple coat on too. She looked like a giant Quality Street sweet.

'Because everyone deserves a souvenir from New York, don't they?' She was a funny one to try and work out sometimes, my great aunt. And I was never quite sure how she was going to react, but I hadn't expected her to wrinkle her nose at the idea that I might want to buy something from Candy Cane Lane

'You can have whatever you want in this shop, Lib, without

having to pay for it.' Aunt Dottie walked across to stand opposite me and fixed me with a determined look. 'But you don't need a souvenir, because I don't want you to go.'

'That's lovely of you to say.' With endearments from my great aunt as sparing as they were, her comment was like warm water washing over me. I knew she meant it – she never said anything she didn't mean – but she must have known it was never going to be possible for me to stay. 'I don't want to go either. I love it here. But I need to be with Nan and Granddad; they're all I've got left of Mum and Dad, and I have to be wherever they are. So I'll be flying back on Christmas Eve, even though being here has felt more like home than I ever thought it could.' The words tripped off my tongue easily, so I had no idea why my throat felt red raw.

'What if I said that this shop was all going to be yours? I want you to have it.' There were tears in her eyes and suddenly panic was gripping my throat too. She must have had bad news, there was no other explanation for it and the idea I might lose her was terrifying.

'Are you okay? Have you been back to the hospital?' My question came out in a rush, but Dottie was already shaking her head.

'I had my check-up, and I'm fighting fit. But having the break from working, after my hip operation, has made me realise I don't want to do this any more. I don't want to work this hard. I never had children of my own, and Ruby's family was the closest I ever had to that. You'd need to give me a wage as a silent partner, until I'm gone, but it would be all yours after that.'

'Oh, Aunt Dottie, no. Don't even talk like that. Candy Cane Lane is you through and through. We get so many people asking after you. There was a guy from Luxembourg just this morning, who said he comes in to buy his wife a new decoration whenever he's over here on business and that you always help him to pick out something she'll love. He was gutted when he realised you weren't working. You can't give up the shop.'

'I can do whatever I bloody well like. I always have and I always will.' It was funny, she lost her New York twang completely when she swore. 'When I moved in here, people said I couldn't name the shop Candy Cane Lane, that I had to make it stand out more by calling it Kandy Kane Lane with a "K". I mean, can you think of anything more ridiculous? I refused to eat Krispy Kremes for years because of the stupid spelling. But then I ate one at Betty's house, without knowing it was a Krispy Kreme, and now I can't bloody stop. Every server in their store on Sixth knows me by name.'

I laughed, and I could only imagine her outrage at being duped into side-lining her principles over the spelling of a dough-nut. 'You do make me laugh, Dottie, but I'm not sure what any of that has to do with the idea of me staying in New York to take over the store.'

'They told me I couldn't name the shop Candy Cane Lane, because it wasn't memorable enough, but I did, and it worked. I just knew it my bones. It's the same when I see you in here; I know it's right for you, and I know it's right for the shop.'

'It's such an amazing offer but I just—'

She cut me off before I could finish. 'Don't give me your answer yet. Wait until the New Year, wait until you've been back in that empty pub for a bit, if you like.'

Just the thought of being back in the pub hurt my heart a little bit. It wasn't that I didn't have a fondness for the regulars, but there was a sadness behind the reason why most of them hung out there so often. They had nothing much to go home to. I'd joked with Nan before my parents' accident, and before I'd ever worked there, that the micro-pub should get a grant for community service. It provided a warm and friendly place for a lot of lonely people, and sometimes I suspected it might be their only conversation of the day. There were four Johns who were regulars, so they had nicknames to differentiate them from one another, but most of the others seemed to have nicknames too. It was something else that gave them a sense of belonging. Everyone from Tarmac Trev, who used to work on the roads, to Bookshelf Steve, who'd run the local library for the last twenty years of his working life. It explained why they'd talk about everything over a pint of real ale, whether it was the mundane, like Railway John's vendetta with the council over a lost wheely bin lid, or the heart-wrenching, like Posh Jan's devastation when her beloved cat Lady Grey had died of cancer.

Working in the shop was so different. Everyone who came in seemed to have a joyful reason for doing so. Whether it was buying a souvenir to remember their trip of a lifetime, choosing a gift for a loved one, or just finding an ornament to add to their collection to help celebrate the upcoming holiday season. I was sure that being surrounded by that sort of joy every day was part of what had helped me shake off the cloak of melancholy I'd worn since my parents' accident. I wanted to remember the past now, but I wanted to embrace the future too and it felt like it would be much harder to do that if I went back to working in my grandparents' pub. Except going home wasn't about the pub, it was about being with Nan and Granddad, and that was something I couldn't imagine ever giving up the chance to do.

'I can't see it changing my answer, but I'll give it to the New Year to think it over, if that's what you want me to do.'

'Great. Just don't rule it out before you've properly considered it, okay?'

'Okay.' Aunt Dottie pulled me into her arms, and I got a mouthful of purple fur from the trim on the hood of her coat. Despite that, it was a moment I'd never forget, for all the right reasons. I might not be able to accept her offer, but it meant a lot,

and it was just another reason why it would be so hard to say
goodbye to New York when the time came.

I could feel the atmosphere in the Community Center as soon as I
walked in. It had always been a place that felt incredibly
welcoming but now there was a coldness, as if bad news had
seeped into the building itself, and, as soon as I saw the others, I
knew there was something seriously wrong. Even the pugs looked
depressed. They weren't hunting around for treats, and they barely
even looked up from their spot on the sofa when I walked in.

'What's wrong?' One glance at Karly's face said it was bad. She
looked as if she might have been crying.

'They're threatening to demolish the building, unless we can
raise half a million dollars to make it safe.' Karly sniffed as Abbie,
who'd been putting up a poster on the noticeboard, put a
comforting arm around her friend.

'You're joking.' Even as I said the words, I wished I could take
them back. This was no laughing matter and when Abbie looked
up at me, there were tears in her eyes too.

'I wish we were. I still can't believe they're going to demolish
the building, but a prime building lot in Manhattan is clearly
worth a lot more to them than everything this place does for the
people who use it. I don't think they realise it's been a life safer for
some of us. Or maybe they do, and they just don't care.'

'Who's threatening to demolish the building?' Whoever it
was, they couldn't do it. Abbie was right, it was a hub of the
community. Not just for the art classes, or as a venue for her
weird theatre performances, either. There was a food bank, and a
crèche for low-income workers, as well as a seniors' club that
Aunt Dottie and Betty both belonged to. Manhattan might be

one of the wealthiest places in the world, but, outside of Midtown, it still had its fair share of issues, and the Community Center helped bridge the gap. In a weird way, it did for some of the residents of this part of New York what my grandparents' micro-pub did for its regulars. It was somewhere they felt welcome, like they belonged, and a place where they'd always find someone to chat to, no matter how lonely the rest of their day might have been.

'The Department of Buildings. They said if we can't raise the money, it's not safe for us to stay open.' Abbie shook her head. 'I've already arranged to stage a play to raise money, and put posters up, but it would be a small miracle if we raised a thousand dollars, never mind half a million.'

'What exactly are they saying is wrong?' I had no expertise to offer, but maybe one of the others would know someone who did. If we could do some of the basics ourselves, we might even be able to save a bit of money.

'It doesn't meet the fire code, and some of the electrics need replacing, but the main issue is the wall from the building that used to be next door.' Karly still looked as if she was in shock. 'It's attached to our building on one side, but other than that it's free-standing, and the guy who came to inspect it said it could fall down at any minute.'

'Shame it didn't fall down on his goddamn head.' Paula came up behind me and I was taken aback by the ferocity of her words. She was usually the most level-headed person in the group.

'It wouldn't have solved the problem, sweetheart, it would just have postponed it.' Deshawn took hold of Paula's hand, and it was obvious their relationship was moving a lot faster than mine and Harry's. They already looked every inch a proper couple and she leant her head against him for a moment, clearly taking comfort in his support, but this must have been devastating for her too. Even though I wouldn't be around to see the result, I really wanted to help.

'Is there anything we can do? Can't we appeal or something, or apply for a grant to help pay for the work?' There had to be something we could do. If I felt as gutted as I did, when I'd be leaving in four weeks, I couldn't even imagine how everyone else was feeling. And maybe there was part of me that wanted to make sure they'd never be able to forget me either. If I could help them hold on to the Community Center, there was a chance they'd remember me as fondly as I knew I was going to remember all of them. I'd spent so much of my energy trying to stop myself from falling in love with Harry, I'd forgotten to stop myself from developing such strong feelings for everyone else. I was even going to miss trying to get dog hair and trails of slobber off my jeans, when one of the pugs decided to show me some affection in the hope of earning a treat. I didn't want to leave any of them behind, but I had no choice. One thing I could do was help them fight to save the Community Center, even if that just meant supporting them with online stuff once I was back home in Canterbury.

'I don't think it's going to be that easy. The guy who came in to do the inspection said there's just no money in the budget for projects like this. But Rob, Dannie and Harry are all up in the studio already, seeing if they can come up with a plan. Although I don't hold out much hope.' Karly rubbed her eyes. She was going to be the most affected of anyone by the closure. This wasn't just the place she came to work every day, it was her home too.

I followed Paula and DeShawn up to the studio, and Harry walked over as we came into the room. 'Was Karly okay when you got here?' I loved that about him – that he seemed to consider everyone's feelings. What I didn't love was the feeling his question stirred up in me. Karly was at risk of losing her home, her job, and the Community Center she loved, and yet a tiny bit of me was jealous of her. Harry obviously cared about Karly, and I knew from Rob that she wasn't dating anyone. Not only that, she'd be in New York after I was long gone. But I hated myself so much for even thinking it. The schoolgirl type behaviour clearly hadn't completely gone away, but I needed to give myself a shake. Everyone had troubles and it was about time I realised that sometimes other people's problems had to take priority over mine.

'She's obviously really upset. I think she's just hoping we can find a solution somehow. I can't imagine how hard this is for her, worrying that the place she calls home might suddenly not be there any more.' I slipped my hand into his, all thoughts of holding him at arm's length temporarily forgotten. The truth was, I had a tiny inkling of how she might be feeling, because the apartment above Candy Cane Lane was starting to feel like that for me. Whenever it was time to leave, I wouldn't say I was going back to the apartment, I'd say I was going home, and it had been that way since the first week I'd arrived. But, unlike Karly, at least I was allowed to make my own choice. Her home was being ripped away from her. A back-up plan in case we couldn't save the Community Center had already popped into my head; maybe I could persuade Aunt Dottie to let Karly take over the shop. She'd have the skills and it would give her a place to live, even if the apartment above Candy Cane Lane wasn't exactly the best place for four pugs to set up home. It was only a few blocks from Central Park, and I'd feel a lot less guilty about turning down Aunt Dottie's offer if I knew she had someone she could rely on to take over. I was still hoping we could save the Community Center, but if I laid some groundwork with my great aunt, in case the worst happened, at least Karly wouldn't find herself homeless and jobless in the New Year.

'This sucks.' Rob looked up from his phone. 'I've been searching every website I can think of to see if we might qualify for funding, but I just keep hitting brick walls.'

'Ironic given that a brick wall's the reason we're in this mess in the first place.' Dannie drummed his fingers on the table. It looked like Karly was right; it wasn't going to be easy to come up with a solution.

'Maybe we could do some fundraising? We could offer to put plaques up on the wall, for people who know and love the Community Center. Or do a reverse brick sponsoring, and get people who've used the services, and who can afford it, to donate.' I didn't know if we had a hope in hell of raising enough money, but we had to try.

'Okay, you're going to have to explain the reverse brick sponsoring to me.' Harry smiled and I wondered for a moment what he'd say if I told him about my aunt's offer to take over the shop. Would he want me to stay?

'My old firm was involved in a project where staff were asked to sponsor a brick, to build a school in Africa. We all paid a hundred pounds for a brick, and it went towards the cost of the building. They put a plaque up with the names of all the sponsors at the end, and we all got a certificate and a picture of our brick.' I laughed at the look that crossed Harry's face, and I didn't blame him. It did sound a bit ridiculous when I said it out loud. But anything was worth a try. 'We could get people to sponsor the safe removal of each brick, which they could keep as a souvenir, and put the money towards the demolition of the old wall and making the electrics safe.'

'I've heard worse ideas.' Harry nodded, and Rob started writing up a list of all the things we could do to raise money.

The rest of the group arrived in dribs and drabs for the art class, and once word spread about the threat of closure, everyone was talking about it.

'I know we should be concentrating on brainstorming ideas, too, but I've been thinking about seeing you again ever since we last met up.' Harry spoke quietly as we stood in the corner of the studio together, watching Dannie and Rob hold court. They seemed to have taken charge of the 'Save the Community Center' campaign and if anyone had a chance of making in happen, it was them.

'Me too.' I took a deep breath. With things getting busier and busier in the shop, there might not be that many more opportunities before I left, especially now we needed to help put our efforts into saving the Community Center. Suddenly my attempts to protect myself by not spending too much time on my own with Harry seemed like a stupid waste. Just because it was going to end, it didn't mean we couldn't make the most of it. It would have been like Paula cancelling the art classes as soon as she'd heard about the plans for the demolition. Even if the campaign to save it failed, I knew for sure she'd run those classes right up until the moment before the wrecking ball was swung if she could, and I needed to follow her example. 'In fact, I was wondering if I could cash in that promise for you to show me a New York Christmas.'

'Just the two of us?'

'If you think you can put up with spending a whole day on your own with me?' I couldn't look at Harry as I said it, so I stared at DeShawn's kaleidoscope painting instead.

'Like I said before, it's what I've been wanting ever since you told me about your obsession with *The Smurfs*.' Harry laughed. I was never going to escape that one; I'd always be the girl who'd admitted to watching the Smurf movie. But it was okay. I wanted Harry to remember something about me when I was gone, even if it was only that.

9

The food kiosks at Bryant Park Winter Village were an assault on the senses, and my stomach rumbled in response.

'What do you fancy?' Harry turned to me as he spoke.

'It all smells so good, I might need a recommendation.'

'The pretzels stuffed with Swiss cheese are pretty unbeatable.' Harry kept hold of my hand as people surged past us on both sides, heading toward the ice rink.

'Sounds good to me.' He was such easy company to be in, and I was so glad I'd decided to take up his offer. My time in New York was a bit like looking inside one of the snow globes, but I was actually inside the bubble – for the next few weeks at least. After that, it would just be a memory that I got out every now and then, but could never go back to. I refused to feel sad about the idea, because my time in the city had taught me that there was nothing more precious than making memories. Not even scum-of-the-earth drunk drivers could take them away. The more memories I had of my stay in New York, and most of all with Harry, the better.

I waited while he ordered the pretzels, and looked up at the huge Christmas tree at one end of the ice rink. He was right, New

Yorkers really knew how to do Christmas. We'd already been to the zoo at Central Park to see the penguins, and there'd been another flurry of snow whilst we were there, making it feel even more like a scene from a Christmas card. Harry had clearly meant what he said about showing me as much of a New York Christmas as he could fit in on one day, too. After we finished at the winter village, we were going on to the market at Grand Central Station, then for a walk to look at the window displays in all the big department stores, before ending up at the Rockefeller Center, to see what Harry promised me would be the best Christmas tree I'd ever laid eyes on. If he was trying to convince me that New York was special, he didn't have to try so hard.

'What do you think?' Harry smiled as I took a bite of the pretzel.

'It's amazing. Honestly, I never knew a pretzel could taste like this. The ones at home are like cardboard in comparison.'

'I don't suppose pretzels – even ones this good – could convince you to stay in New York?'

'Let me get back to you on that!' I didn't want to get into a conversation about going home. This was my perfect snow globe day, and reality definitely wasn't allowed in.

'So, what do you eat in England at Christmas?'

'Mince pies, Christmas cake, Christmas pudding.' I laughed. 'There's a lot of dried fruit involved, now I come to think of it.'

'Maybe I should give that a try. I've always wanted to go to England, and Canterbury is definitely on my wish list to visit.'

'Really?' I was surprised he'd even heard of the small city where I'd been born and raised. Not that we didn't have lots of tourists, but, if I'd had to choose between Christmas with a view of the Empire State Building, or carols at Canterbury Cathedral – as beautiful as that was in its own way – there'd be no contest for me. New York had got me, hook, line and sinker.

'I studied *The Canterbury Tales* at high school and, unlike almost everyone else, I quite enjoyed it.' Harry's expression wasn't entirely convincing. 'But even if I wasn't a total geek who finds medieval pilgrims fascinating, you'd be there. So why wouldn't I want to visit?'

'Well I could always introduce you to the delights of real ale at my grandparents' pub. It's only fair after you've shown me how good these pretzels are.'

'So real ale's good?'

'Well, some people love it. And if you genuinely enjoyed reading *The Canterbury Tales*, then I think you could handle it!'

'And you're really going home on Christmas Eve?' Harry wasn't the first person to ask me that question, with a look on his face that suggested it was something only a mad woman would do.

'With the time difference, I'll be arriving in the afternoon and checking into a hotel, until I can get the train home. Missing Christmas like that makes it easier to deal with. When I agreed with Nan that I'd come out here, flying back on Christmas Eve was the only way I could cope with the idea. I couldn't bear the thought of being here for the holidays without my parents.' I still didn't want to let the real world in, or put a dampener on Harry's attempt to make me feel Christmassy, but I couldn't lie to him either. I was learning to love the run-up to Christmas, New York style. Even without Harry's intervention, I could hardly avoid it working in Candy Cane Lane. But I still couldn't bear the thought of a *real* Christmas Day. As wonderful as it had been to relive some of the memories from my childhood, Christmas would never be the same again without one of Dad's festive breakfasts, where the pancakes were cut into the shape of Christmas trees and some- where along the line orange juice had given way to bucks fizz. I'd never wake up on Christmas morning again to find Mum excitedly hovering by the Christmas stockings, which she'd left downstairs the night before, and still pretending – right up to my last Christmas with them – that she had no idea what they contained. I could do all those things myself, but without Mum and Dad, it would just be a poor imitation. That's why the run-up to Christmas in New York had been so good for me. There'd been no traditions I needed to keep, where the absence of my parents would be thrown into even starker contrast than usual. But I couldn't stay here for Christmas either, or create new traditions, like always ordering the Swiss cheese bagel from Bryant Park. So an overnight flight from New York and twenty-four hours in a soulless airport hotel was as good as it was going to get.

'Why don't you just stay on until the end of the year?' Harry's dark brown eyes searched my face, and he was in danger of letting reality stamp all over our plans for the day. 'It's only a few more days. What difference would it make?'

'It would just make it harder.' I didn't want to give Aunt Dottie any false hope by staying on, even for another week. She'd already started rubbing her hip and saying she was pretty sure she'd need the other one replacing before long, even though I knew for a fact that she and Brian had signed up for beginners' swing dancing classes in the New Year. Despite that, I hated the idea of leaving the shop and I really wanted to stay around and help save the Community Center. There were so many reasons to stay, but an even bigger reason to leave. We weren't a religious family, but on New Year's Day we always had a family walk after lunch that took us through the churchyard where my parents had got married, and where their ashes were now buried. I'd been christened there too and it was even where my parents had met, at an after-school youth club, run by a forward-thinking vicar who believed the church should be at the heart of the community. Dad would stop us outside the building every New Year's Day and say something about how the biggest events in his life were linked to that place.

He'd tell us what he hoped the New Year was going to bring and ask us to do the same.

'New Year's resolutions are always broken by the middle of January, but this really works.' Dad would lift up crossed fingers as he spoke, and I'd laugh every time at the way he seamlessly combined superstition with some kind of belief in a more powerful force. Whatever his logic, or lack of it, those New Year's days were another of our traditions. I knew how much it meant to Dad for me to be there and, wherever I'd seen in midnight the evening before, I'd make sure I got back to Canterbury in time for our afternoon walk every first of January. So, the idea of not being with them, in that churchyard on New Year's Day, was unthinkable.

Harry reached out and touched my hand. 'I'm still hoping that today might change things.'

'Thank you so much for arranging all of this. I'm having so much fun.' It didn't matter what else Harry showed me, it wouldn't change my mind. But telling him that he was wasting his time would have killed the mood stone dead. Instead, I leant forward and kissed him, knowing I'd never forget what it felt like to be in Harry's arms. I was just making memories after all, and surely one day of make-believe couldn't do too much damage.

* * *

'Has the market given you any ideas for the shop?' Harry didn't push me any more about going home as we walked on through the winter village. It was one of the things that continually amazed me about him – that he knew just when to back off. The ice rink was lined with kiosks, which looked a bit like Victorian greenhouses, and it must have been even more magical in the evening. But Harry wanted to be at the Rockefeller Center when it got dark, to see the tree in all its glory, and then we were going ice skating back in Central Park. But it was me who wanted *that* part of the day to be in the dark. The less light there was on me when I was skating, the better, and I had a horrible feeling I was going to humiliate myself. Especially as Harry had said he had his own skates. Some people had natural balance, but I wasn't one of them. It was only due to Dad's perseverance that I ever learned to ride a bike. I managed straight lines quite quickly, but as soon as I tried to turn anything resembling a corner, my bike would go one way and I'd go the other. So, the chances of me being able to stay upright, balancing on blades on a rink of ice, were almost zero. My only hope was that they'd have some of those penguin skating aids to lean on. If it came down to it, I wasn't averse to the idea of wrestling one from a five-year-old. They were much closer to the ground than me anyway.

'There are some lovely wooden ornaments on a couple of the stalls, and I've picked up some business cards so that Dottie can contact them in the New Year.' There was nothing as beautiful as the snow globes, though, and I had to be strict with myself about buying too much stuff that I'd have to ship home. It was pointless buying tree decorations, anyway. We had a tree in the micro-pub, but my grandparents came from an era where it was impossible to have enough tinsel. So traditionally hand-crafted wooden ornaments would have been wasted.

My grandparents hadn't put up a tree, in the flat above the pub, the Christmas after my parents had died – which was almost certainly more for my benefit than theirs. Sometimes I marvelled at their ability to keep going after losing their daughter. I knew it wasn't because they'd loved Mum any less than I did, but a year after the accident their smiles began to look less painted on and I started hearing them laugh again. When I questioned Nan about it, she said she knew that's what Mum would have wanted and that she felt as though she could hear Mum's voice sometimes, urging her to get up and get on with life, because wallowing in sadness wouldn't change anything. I would have given anything to hear Mum's voice again, even if it was only Nan's imagination talking. Since I'd got to New York, I'd started to understand what Nan meant far more clearly. I didn't need to buy a suitcase full of decorations to remind me of what I'd found in the city, or to remember how wonderful Christmases with my parents had been, because New York had unlocked those memories for me too. I had the little tree in the snow globe and I didn't need anything else. Which meant that tree decorations were nowhere near the top of my shopping list – from Candy Cane Lane, or anywhere else.

'I've seen a couple of decorations I might get for my mom and sister.' Harry picked up his mobile phone. 'And my nephews have sent a list as long as my arm of the toys they want from Macy's. If I do decide to fly across to San Francisco, I'll have to work out what I can actually take. Although, if I shop early enough, I could get it sent out. I'll have to do that, anyway, if I decide not to head west for the holidays.'

'You're not definitely going to your sister's for Christmas then?'

'It depends.'

'On what?'

'On you.' I had to hand it to Harry – he might not push too hard, but he didn't give up easily either.

'Maybe we should start at Macy's then, and you can get your order in.' I'd almost said *just in case*. But there was no *just in case* and I think even Harry knew that deep down. Maybe he wanted that snow globe moment as much as I did.

'Sounds good.' Harry took my hand again and we wandered back into the crowd, merging with everyone else. I must have looked like a normal tourist wanting nothing more than to soak in the festive atmosphere and, just for one day, I was determined to feel like one, too.

* * *

'They look gorgeous, don't they? I had no idea people could get married at the Rockefeller Center.' The newlywed couple, and a small group of guests, were posing for pictures by the Christmas tree. There seemed to be millions of Christmas trees in New York, and a lot of the other trees, which were mostly bare of their leaves, were wrapped in lights, too. It was almost as if every tree in New York became a Christmas tree for the holidays. But nothing came close to the Rockefeller tree. It lived up to all the hype.

Like so much of New York, I'd seen it on screen. As I stood there next to Harry, I could picture the moment when Kevin and his mum meet at the tree on Christmas Eve, in *Home Alone 2,* as clearly as if they were standing right next to me. Mum and I had watched that movie together every year when I was growing up, and I could almost hear the sound of her laughter as I looked up. The tree was so beautiful too, with thousands of multi-coloured lights, and a huge gold star on the top, which, by itself, was probably as tall as Harry.

'I'm not sure that you can actually get married here, but I know a lot of people come here to pose for pictures, especially at this time of year.' Harry was smiling as he watched the couple and I suddenly found myself wondering if he'd ever come close to a moment like that. For all I knew, he could have been married before. Maybe he still was. There was so much that I didn't know and yet I'd felt an instant connection to him that somehow meant I'd trusted a total stranger, that first day in the park, with my deepest secret.

'Are you married?' The question came straight out in the end.

'No.' Harry laughed, as if it was the most absurd thing he'd ever been asked, but I'd have bet there were plenty of past girl-friends who'd imagined what it would be like to be married to him, or at least imagined building a life with Harry. I'd only known him for a month and, if I let myself, I could picture it too. It was a Sunday morning for me – the two of us grabbing breakfast from Dannie and Rob's deli, before taking a long walk in the park, or catching the subway out to Coney Island and holding hands as we wandered along the boardwalk.

Harry stop laughing as he looked at me, a serious expression crossing his face. 'Have *you* got something to tell me? Is there a husband or a boyfriend back in England you forgot to mention?'

'No, and looking back now, I'm not sure I've ever really been in love before.' I'd hated Ryan when he left, for abandoning me when I'd needed someone most, but he'd done the right thing for both of us. I didn't love him, at least not in the way you were supposed to love someone you wanted to share your life with. The pain of losing him didn't even register in the wake of my parents' accident, but my throat felt raw when I thought about the fact that I'd prob-ably never see Harry again once I headed back home. If I already felt his loss so keenly after such a short time together, it proved what Ryan and I had shared hadn't even compared.

'Me neither. Not yet anyway.' Harry put a hand under my chin, forcing me to look up at him, but the vulnerability that came with being able to really feel things again was suddenly terrifying.

'You don't have to say that. This is... we're not...' I couldn't finish the sentence, because despite the urge to protect myself, it was impossible to pass this off as nothing.

'I'm not saying anything because I think I have to. I don't know what this is, but I know what I'd want it to be if you were staying. You might not believe me, but I've never felt as though I've known someone from before I even met them, the way I did with you.'

Harry smiled. 'God, that sounds like a line from a song. Hell, it might even be a line from a song for all I know, but that doesn't make it any less true.'

'If I was staying, I might even tell you that I feel the same way.' It was as close as I could bear to get to confessing the truth. 'But I can't stay, and sometimes not saying things can be for the best. It makes the goodbyes easier.'

'I can't see anything making the goodbyes easier for me, but I don't want to think about that right now. You promised me the whole day, remember?'

'I did and I don't want to forget a single second of it.' Leaning into Harry, I tried to focus on the here and now, looking up at the lights on the tree in front of me, instead of already starting to picture the moment I'd walk away from him for the final time. Mum and Dad would have loved the tree so much. They'd run a landscaping business together, which they'd finally started a year or so before they'd died, and the pinnacle of my dad's dream was to set up a Christmas tree farm. He'd had his eye on the perfect piece of land, which he'd said he was going to make an offer on, as soon as they had enough money from the business. They'd worked such long hours to make it a success, and it was another reason I'd so wanted them to have the break in New York. Central Park would have been like heaven to them, too. That same thought was what had made me dissolve into tears the first time I'd seen Harry in the park, but I didn't feel like crying for what they were missing on this trip any more. Somewhere along the line, I'd realised it was Mum who'd been guiding me since I got to the city. We'd spoken countless times about the things she was going to do when she and Dad finally got to visit, and it was following her plan that meant I'd got to see so much of the city in my time off from the shop. I still wished she could have been there with me, but now I could see how happy both my parents were right up until the end. They'd found someone they adored in one another, and I'd always known that raising me was the thing that had made them happiest of all. They'd been able to set up their dream business and they'd had so much fun planning the trip to New York. Grant Bailey had taken away their lives, but I couldn't let him take away everything that had gone before. And I wasn't going to let him take away the time I had left in New York either.

I turned to Harry and he pulled me towards him. I had a feeling that the more I knew about him, the harder it would be to walk away when the time came, but I still wanted to find out as much as I could before it was too late. 'Is this your favourite place at Christmas, then?'

'No, I love it, but Central Park has always been my favourite place, whatever time of year. And now that it's the place I met you, it's going to be even more special.'

I leant my head against his shoulder, allowing myself another moment that I'd lock into my memory. The couple in front of us were still having photographs taken and quite a crowd had gathered, some of them taking pictures of their own. It was strange to think that this couple might be appearing in other people's social media posts.

'I'm not sure I'd want to pose for photos with this many people looking at me.' I pulled away from Harry. 'Not that I'll ever get married.'

'Never?' Harry eyes were searching my face again. It might seem like an unusual conversation to be having on our first proper date, but then my encounters with Harry had never quite worked out how I would have planned.

'I couldn't get married without my parents there.'

'That must be tough, but don't you think they will be there?' Harry's eyes met mine again and it was like he could read my mind, because the exact same thought had popped into my head the moment I'd given him my reason for not wanting to get married. Up until a month ago, I'd have been certain I could never have a wedding without Mum and Dad there, but Harry was right. They'd been with me the whole time I was here and they would continue to be, wherever I was and whatever I did.

'Now that I think about it, you're right, but until I came here I couldn't see that. It's hard for me to imagine myself as a bride, though, maybe because no one's ever come close to asking me!' It was my turn to laugh. 'I don't think it's crossed anyone's mind to think of me that way either. I've always been less of a Miss Right, and more of a Miss Right Now.'

'I find that hard to believe.' Harry turned away from me, so I couldn't see the look on his face. That was the trouble with playing make-believe, it turned out that you couldn't do it, even for a day, unless you wanted to avoid talking about the future altogether. Explaining that I couldn't take things between us any further because my days in New York were numbered was the easy part. After all, distance was a tangible barrier, and there was clear logic as to why a relationship where the couple lived three and a half thousand miles apart might not work. Telling him that I couldn't imagine starting a real relationship with him, even if we lived in the same city, would be a lot harder for him to understand. But I knew better than anyone that loving someone came with a price. Yet, even as I thought it, I realised that Harry was the only person I'd met since my parents' death who I'd even have considered paying that price for. I didn't want him to know that though, so it was far easier to go back to my default habit and change the subject altogether.

'Do you think your nephews will be happy with the toys you chose for them?' I could barely remember what he'd ordered. There'd been so many people in the store – moving around the toy department had been like riding a wave – but somehow Harry had found the things he'd needed and arranged for them to be shipped straight to his sister's house. The window displays in Macy's and the other big stores, like Saks and Bloomingdale's, were stunning. I wondered what Harry would think if he saw the huge foil decorations that would be hanging from the ceiling at the pub back home. Nan must have had them since before I was born, and I spent the whole of December weaving in and out them to avoid getting static shock in my hair. They were tacky, but looking in the window of Macy's, I suddenly missed them.

Grand Central Station had been beautiful too. The ceilings making it feel as though we were standing under a night sky, and there was a choir singing carols at the top of one of the staircases as we passed through. I couldn't help wondering if everyone was as happy as they looked, or if there were other people, like me, just trying to have one perfect day and desperately trying to avoid thinking about what the New Year might bring. There was every chance it would be the year when Grant Bailey was released for good.

'The toys were all on the very long lists they compiled, so I think I might qualify for a *good uncle award* this year.' Harry frowned. 'Although, according to my sister, I actually have to spend Christmas Day with them to even get on the shortlist.'

'You should book your flight.'

'There's no hurry.' Harry looked at his watch. 'Although we are going to have to get going, if we want to make our slot at the ice rink.' He took my hand in his again, and I followed him reluctantly. Partly because I didn't want to leave the tree, but mainly because going back to Central Park was the last thing on our list, and I didn't want the day to end.

As we walked past the wedding party, the bride was being photographed with two people, who I assumed were her parents. The older woman was in a wheelchair, and the bride sat on the armrest of it, with her arm around her mother's shoulders, and her father holding her around the waist. I caught the bride's eye, as we walked right behind the photographer, and smiled. I hope she realised how lucky she was and took every chance she could to make memories with her parents. I'd be forever thankful that I'd somehow had the foresight to do that, and I was also incredibly grateful for the time I'd spent in New York, which had allowed me to see just how precious those memories were.

* * *

'You're not as bad at this as you made out.' Harry was gliding across the ice on the rink in Central Park, with me clinging to his arm like a giant koala bear. I must have laid it on pretty thick if this was better than he'd expected.

'If you let go of me, I'll be on my bum in all of about five seconds.'

'I won't ever let go of you, I promise.' I stared down at the ice as Harry spoke. He didn't seem to be the sort to say things he didn't mean, but I'd be gone soon and it could just have been his way of trying to get me into bed. Although he didn't seem like the sort of person to employ that kind of manipulation either and, however rubbish I might be at skating, I wasn't naïve enough to fall for a line designed to get me naked. But maybe I could be the sort of girl who'd say yes to spending the night with Harry, knowing it would be a one-time thing, just this once. I might regret it if I did, especially if it made saying goodbye even harder. But I had a feeling I'd regret it even more if I didn't.

The earlier snowfall had settled, and every hour or so, there'd be another heavy flurry. I couldn't remember ever having a white Christmas, and that was another pull to stay in New York. Harry had asked me to stay, and I knew if I did, he'd make sure I didn't spend Christmas alone. Dannie and Rob had offered to host me too, and I'd found myself wondering, even as I tried to stay upright on the ice, whether maybe I could delay my return home for just a few days. I'd made so much progress in focusing on the good times with my parents that the idea of actually celebrating Christmas was no longer unthinkable. But if I had the perfect Christmas in New York, I was scared it might make me want to stay even more. I had to go home to spend New Year's Day with my parents, in the only way I could, and leaving before Christmas felt safer. It had taken me almost two years to feel like I had the right to smile again, and I didn't want a perfect New York Christmas to ruin that. If nothing back home could compare to that experience, I was terrified it might mean I'd forget how to smile again. I couldn't risk it, any more than I could risk letting my feelings for Harry deepen even further.

'Hey, I didn't know you two were skating as well tonight,' Rob called out as he and Dannie skated over to us.

'Harry's skating, I'm just slowing him down.'

Dannie kissed me on both cheeks and I nearly brought Harry down onto the ice with me as a result.

'So, how's it going? Condensing Christmas in New York into a single day?' Rob had a woolly hat on, with reindeers running around the side, but somehow he still managed to look cool.

'It's been brilliant.' I turned to Harry. 'I couldn't have asked for a better guide, or better company.'

'Ooh, do I hear wedding bells?' Dannie grinned. If he had his way, he'd have me married off to Harry by the New Year, if it meant I wouldn't be going back home to the pub.

'Just Christmas bells.' I gave Dannie a look. He was a hopeless romantic. It was hardly surprising, given the strength of his relationship with Rob. But I'd only known Harry for six weeks, and even if I had been staying, Dannie was running way ahead of himself.

'I've got one more surprise actually, and we're gonna have to leave you guys to own the ice rink, I'm afraid.' Harry laughed – he didn't take himself too seriously – even though he seemed to be good at everything he did.

'Are you going to the Community Center tomorrow?' Rob pulled his hat down over his ears; the temperature seemed to be dropping by the moment. 'Karly wants to talk about the fundraising, to see if there's any chance of us making the target. She's talking about us doing a calendar too.'

'What? One of those with a strategically placed fireman's helmet?' Dannie grinned. 'Or you could have a pecan pie, darling!'

'It's not that sort of calendar.' Rob wrinkled his nose. 'At least I hope not.'

'We'll be there.' I gave Rob a hug, and Harry had to rescue me again, as my feet seemed determined to skate off without the rest of me. I didn't let go of him until we got to the edge of the ice. I might never have admitted it, even to myself, but having to cling on to Harry so tightly had been the best part of an already amazing day.

'You don't really think Karly's going to want us to pose in the nude for a calendar, do you?' I sucked in my stomach, thinking about the Swiss cheese pretzel that had been joined by candied nuts, hot chocolate piled high with cream and topped with shavings of chocolate truffle, and the meatball sliders that Harry said I just had to try. I'd also spent the last six weeks living next door to Rob and Dannie, who were always bringing me things around to try, and pastries from the deli that I just had to eat because they wouldn't last. I don't think my body had ever been less calendar ready, and if it hadn't been for the long walks and less-frequent jogs in Central Park, I might have needed to book two seats on the plane home. As it was, I was still just about managing to do up my jeans, but it was getting to the stage where I had to lie on the bed to zip them up. I loved the clothes sizing in America, though. I'd never been a size ten in my adult life, but I was in the States. It was almost a good enough reason to stay on its own.

'Knowing Karly, it's more likely to be a calendar with the pugs featuring every month instead of any of us.' Harry had already changed his boots, and he took mine off me to return to the rental stand. 'Although I think Dannie might actually be disappointed.'

'So, am I allowed to ask what this final surprise is?' I put my arm through Harry's after he'd returned my skates and put his in one of the lockers. I couldn't imagine what he could possibly have arranged that would make this day any better, but he was looking pretty confident as he tapped the side of his nose.

'Let's just say that your carriage awaits.'

'Really? Like in the films?' I'd always wanted to do a carriage ride through the park and it had definitely been on Mum's wish list too. But it was one of those things – like a gondola ride – that felt like you needed to do it with the person you loved, or at least the person you were romantically involved with.

'I know it's a cliché, but it wouldn't be a New York Christmas without one.' Harry led me towards the edge of the park, where the horses and carriages were lined up, and couples went past us covered with blankets. I didn't care if some people thought it was a cliché, it was the perfect end to a perfect day.

'This is Toby.' Harry gestured towards the carriage driver, who tipped his hat in response. 'And that's Sam, the best horse in Central Park.' I stepped up into the white covered carriage, and Harry sat down beside me, pulling the deep red blanket over our knees, as Sam and Toby set off into the park.

'This is like a fairy tale. No wonder you never wanted to leave New York after college.'

'Like I said before, it has a way of getting under your skin. I knew, after the first few days here, that I was home, even though I was born and grew up on the West Coast.' Harry put his arm around my shoulder. 'Some places are like that and, if you're really lucky, some people are too.'

'What was the name of your college again?' There was no point us going over old ground. It might have hurt Harry that I kept glossing over his comments, but it was easier than admitting that I felt the same way. I'd already told Harry I felt as though I'd known him for years, so I just wanted to talk about nothing much at all. It might be one of my last chances to find out all the things I wanted to know about him too.

'Parsons School of Design. I wanted to go to the New York Academy of Art originally, but I didn't get in. Now I'm so glad I didn't, otherwise I'd never have met Paula.' Harry's face was shadowed in the darkness, but I wanted to read his expression. Paula seemed really happy with DeShawn, but there was still a part of me that wondered if there was more than friendship between her and Harry, even if it was in the past. I had no right to let it bother me, but it did.

'And you lived together?'

'Yes, we hit it off in our first semester, and after that we rented a brownstone together in Greenwich Village. It belonged to her godfather, and the rent we paid was ridiculously low, otherwise we'd never have afforded it.'

'Was she in a wheelchair then?'

'No, and she fought it every step of the way too, but I admire her so much. She's achieved ten times more than me, and she's still surprising people who were stupid enough to try and write her off. If anyone can save the Community Center, it'll be her.'

'And were the two of you ever more than... you know, friends?' It was a simple enough question, but I was still tripping over the words. I was prying into a life that very soon I wouldn't be part of, but I couldn't seem to stop myself.

'No, she was dating someone else when we first met and, by the time she was single again, we were such good friends that I didn't look at her in that way. She's my best friend.'

'I know you said you've never been in love, but surely that can't mean you've always been single?'

'There were a few girls during the college years, but no one serious. And I've had my share of dates since then, but only one relationship that ever felt like it was going to go somewhere.'

'What happened?'

'She was a middle school teacher I met when she brought her class to one of my talks.'

I tried to rationalise the stabbing sensation in the pit of my stomach at the thought of Harry having another relationship that had started in Central Park. It was ridiculous, he'd worked there for years – of course he'd met other women there. But it felt like *our* place to me and suddenly the idea that as soon as I went home he'd meet someone new there, seemed all the more likely. 'We dated for three years and then we moved in together, but within three months it was over.'

'I'm sorry.'

'I'm not. It wasn't because either of us had habits that the other couldn't stand, or because we couldn't have rubbed along together for the rest of our lives. But I realised that's all we we'd be doing – rubbing along together. And it wasn't enough for me. I didn't think it should be enough for her either. I knew then that I didn't love her the way I'd thought I did, because the idea of letting her go was better than the idea of staying together.'

'Could she see it was the right thing for both of you, too?'

'She was upset, but she married the principal of her school within a year. So, I guess I'm pretty easy to get over when it comes down to it.' Harry laughed in that easy, self-deprecating way he did, and I just hoped he was right, because I already knew I was going to miss him. 'So, what about you, any serious relationships, even if you haven't been in love?'

'I thought I was in one when my parents died and back then I thought I loved him, but I withdrew from everything after that and apparently I was no fun any more. I must be pretty easy to get over too, as he took one of the girls we used to work with to Thailand at Easter and we only split up in the March. Look at us, what a pair of catches. Never been in love and never had anyone love us either by the sounds of things!'

'He might have moved on, but I doubt he'll ever *really* get over you. I've got a feeling that would be very hard to do.' Harry leant towards me and I slid my hands into his dark brown hair, pulling his face closer to mine. We were so close, I could see the flecks of gold in his eyes as we passed by one of the street lamps in the park. The kiss was much more certain this time and I didn't want it to stop there.

'Have you got tea at your apartment?' The words I whispered, after the kiss, hardly qualified for the most romantic sentence in the world, but I was hoping Harry would read between the lines.

'Dannie gave me some of his Yorkshire teabags. He said it's the only tea worth drinking.' He gave me one of his funny looks, obviously wondering how I'd segued from the best kiss I'd ever had in my life, to discussing the merits of Yorkshire tea. It was no good; I was going to have to spell it out.

'Can I come back to your apartment, *with you*?' It would have seemed wrong to take him back to Aunt Dottie's place, and I couldn't risk Dannie and Rob seeing us going in together, or Dannie would be straight down to Bloomingdale's to register us for china.

'For tea?'

'Tea and whatever else takes your fancy.' If I could have hidden my face underneath the blanket I would have done. None of this was like me, and I was cringing inside, but it was what I wanted and time was running out.

'Do you mean that?'

'Yes.'

'In that case, there's nothing I'd like better.' Harry pulled me towards him again, and I knew for certain it was the right thing to do. I'd already had a perfect day and I had a feeling I was about to have the perfect night in New York too. After that, I'd go home and life would go back to the new normal it had fallen into since my parents' accident.

Only I had no idea just how difficult going back would be.

10

'So where are we up to with the fundraising?' Karly was looking around the table expectantly.

'My groups' performances have raised over eight hundred dollars.' Abbie handed out some more flyers. This time the actors were dressed as giant eyeballs. 'This is our next one; it's about the authorities invading our privacy. I've set up a checking account too, so we can all start paying our funds in and make payments out for the most essential works, as soon as we can.'

'I've started doing some private family tours of New York, and I'm getting close to my first thousand dollars.' I had no idea that Harry had already started fundraising and as he spoke, he was holding my hand under the table. We'd agreed to try and keep the progress of our relationship just between the two of us. The last thing I needed was for the others to know and put more pressure on me to stay, because I wanted to more than ever now. I just had to keep telling myself that when my grandparents got back from the cruise, they'd need me in the pub and, even if I could find a way around that, I couldn't leave the city where my parents' ashes were buried, in the churchyard that had been such a special place for us. 'They're aimed at what the kids want to hear about New York. I take them to the Museum of Natural History to talk about *Night at the Museum*, and we follow the *Home Alone 2* trail and things like that. Sometimes we even go up to Belvedere Castle and talk about *The Smurfs*.' Harry caught my eye and laughed.

'That sounds brilliant.' Karly beamed in his direction, and I wanted to say that I thought he was brilliant too, but I seemed to have lost the power of speech. I'd thought my Christmas date with Harry had been perfect. But it wasn't the date that was perfect, it was him. When'd he'd looked at me, laughing at our private joke about *The Smurfs*, I'd felt that connection to him quadruple. This wasn't the way it was supposed to go. I'd told myself over and over again that this was only a fleeting thing, thinking that would somehow protect me from getting in too deep, but I was officially an idiot. Nothing had been able to protect me from falling for Harry.

'I'm probably enjoying it as much as the kids. I'd do it for nothing anyway, so raising money for the Community Center is just a bonus.' He squeezed my hand under the table and I let out a long breath. Taking things an hour at a time was how I'd coped with losing my parents in the end, because looking towards any kind of future without them had seemed so overwhelming. I was just going to have to do the same with Harry, otherwise I was going to miss out on the time we did have left. Some of the tension finally left my shoulders and I realised he was still looking at me. 'Are you going to tell them about what you've been doing in the shop, Libby?'

'My aunt's donating 50 per cent of all the personalised engraving money to the fund.' It sounded pathetic compared to what Harry and Abbie had been doing. 'And I'm running a prize draw, too, for the big Swarovski Christmas decoration, selling tickets at a dollar each. I've sold about two hundred so far.'

'Yeah, and most of those are to Dannie!' Rob rolled his eyes. 'We're holding a charity night at the deli, but Dannie's still up for the calendar idea.'

'I think it's going to be too tight to try and get a calendar printed this year, unfortunately.' Karly lifted one of the pugs onto her lap as she spoke.

'And I've been doing sit-ups all week too!' Dannie grinned. 'So what about you, Paula? Have you been up to much, or have you been too busy analysing DeShawn's *mind*?'

'Actually' – Paula put her hand over DeShawn's – 'we've been very busy fundraising. DeShawn's sold some pictures, and we've been planning an art jam.'

'An art jam?' Maybe it was an American thing, but I already knew it had nothing to do with the stuff I spread on my toast.

'It's a bit like a music jam. We get a load of artists together, doing street art, and we auction off the pieces during the day. It's a street art festival, I guess you'd say.' DeShawn dragged his eyes away from Paula for just long enough to explain. It might have taken her forever to realise he was interested, but surely even she couldn't doubt it now.

'Sounds brilliant; we definitely need to jump on the Parsy bandwagon,' Dannie said. 'I almost had to queue up to get under the Greywacke Arch this week, with the amount of people who'd stopped to look at it, so I reckon that will go down really well.'

'Maybe we could do some street food to sell on the day, too?' Rob looked at Karly, who nodded back.

'Definitely. We really need to push hard if we're going to raise enough money to secure the rest as a loan. I think even I've given up wishing we could raise the whole amount by ourselves in time.'

'I think we should set a date for it, one that we can all make, before it gets too close to Christmas to fit it in. Where's Madison lately, anyway?' Abbie glanced up from the calendar on her phone.

'New boyfriend.' I shrugged my shoulders. 'But he's in the fire department. And she's roped him, and the rest of his firehouse, into doing some snow clearing of sidewalks and driveways to raise money. So she's still doing her bit.'

'Sounds like just the sort of charity work I could get involved with.' Rob laughed, earning himself a pointed look from Dannie.

'How about the twentieth for the art jam then?' Abbie looked up again, and everyone checked their phones. They were a few things people would have to move, but nothing that couldn't be rearranged, so Karly added it to the list. I still wasn't sure if we'd have enough to secure the loan, but we were doing all we could, and that sense of belonging just kept growing. I couldn't imagine not being around to help after Christmas, but at least I'd get to go to the art jam. And maybe learning to count small blessings would turn out to be another step on the road to building a new life for myself again, after I went home. I was starting to hope so.

* * *

'Oh Nan, I do miss you.' I smiled at the screen. It was great seeing her, but in some ways it was harder than just hearing her voice. Although now that she'd finally got to grips with FaceTime, there was no going back to the phone for her.

'We miss you too, Lib.' Nan blew me a kiss. 'But Dottie tells me you're still spending a lot of time with your new friends.'

'I am, and we're busy raising money to keep the Community Center open.' Would I really be back in the pub in less than two weeks? It didn't seem possible. 'What about you, are you all packed for the cruise?'

'We are, and Granddad's even agreed to replace the Speedos he's had since 1972!'

'That definitely counts as a Christmas miracle!'

'He's already looking at brochures for more cruises, too. If this one goes well, there's a four-month round-the-world trip he's got his eye on. Would you believe it?' Nan raised her eyebrows, and the back of my neck prickled. I wasn't sure I could survive leaving New York *and* having to run the pub without my grandparents. It was probably all just talk, though. Granddad would never leave his beloved pub for that long.

'So what else is going on? Is everything okay at the pub?'

'Yes love, it's all fine, but there's something else.' The tone of Nan's voice changed, and she bit her lip.

'What's wrong? Are you both okay?' If either of them were sick, I'd have to go straight home. An image of Harry standing in Central Park flitted into my brain, and I squeezed my eyes shut for a second.

'We're fine. It's just that Granddad saw Grant Bailey. He's definitely been out on home release.'

My eyes shot open again and all the bitterness I seemed to have managed to push down over the last six weeks came bubbling back to the surface. 'I still can't believe it. It's been less than two years and he gets to just pick up where he left off.'

'I know darling.' Nan's eyes had taken on a glassy sheen. 'But like I said before, it wouldn't bring them back if they locked him up forever and threw away the key. Even if that's what he deserves.'

'People need to be reminded of what he's done, so he gets as hard a time as possible.' My scalp prickled at the thought of him strutting around Canterbury, acting as if he hadn't taken two lives and ruined so many others. There'd been an outcry locally at the time of his conviction about the leniency of his sentence, but people had short memories and their own troubles to do deal with. Grant Bailey's life should be the one that was ruined, and if it meant me putting up posters around town to remind people of what he'd done, I was more than prepared to do it. I'd let him get away with this once and I wasn't going to do it again. 'Is Granddad okay? That must have been a horrible shock. Bailey didn't try to speak to him, did he?'

'He hasn't got the guts. For all his cockiness, Granddad said Bailey just stared at the ground. But I think it's just as well we're going on that cruise, because it took all your granddad had to not go over and punch the stupid smirk off Bailey's face once and for all.'

'I wish someone would.' I didn't want it to be Granddad though. He was in his seventies and he should be enjoying life, going on cruises and whatever else he and Nan wanted to do, maybe even looking forward to his first great-grandchild. But because of Grant Bailey, all our plans for the future had changed two years ago. I might have found it hard to get my head around the fact that my grandparents were finally taking a holiday from the pub, but I was even happier now that they were. There'd have been absolutely no chance of them enjoying Christmas with the prospect of bumping into Bailey while he was out celebrating his home release.

'With the circles he moves in, he'll upset the wrong person one day. Billy heard a rumour that he's planning to go to London as soon as he's got the choice. One of his brothers is already up there and a friend of the family said he's made some connections in prison, which mean a move to London would make sense. I hate to even think what they meant by that. But at least he won't be here.' Nan sighed. 'In the meantime, I'm really glad you're over there, because being as far away as possible from him is the best place you could be. I don't want you to come back. At least not yet.'

'I'm not sure how to take that.'

'Yes, you are.' Nan smiled. 'You've been the light of our lives from the moment you were born, Lib, and it's been terrible seeing you change in front of our eyes these last two years. I kept hoping and praying that you'd find something to bring back our sparky girl. You always wanted to fight for what was right, and not just in your job. I know you wanted to do that with Bailey too and for him to get the sentence he deserved. When he didn't, I was scared you were the one who was going to end up with a life sentence of unhappiness. But every time I've spoken to you since you got to New York, I've sensed that light inside of you coming back on little by little. And I think you've found the thing that's giving you back your spark. So, I want you to promise me you'll consider Dottie's offer to take over the shop.'

'She told you?' I should have known. They'd cooked up the plan to get me out to New York in the first place, so it shouldn't have been a surprise to learn that Nan was in on Dottie's plan to get me to stay too.

'She did, and she wants you to stay on so much. Almost as much as I do. And I know that's what your mum would have wanted, too, if she was here. I can almost hear her shouting at you to take this chance. She loved New York, but most of all she loved you. Don't let misplaced guilt stop you from staying, because I know you're happier out there than you've been here since we lost them.'

'I just don't know if I can stay.' I shook my head. But then I thought about Grant Bailey again, and I found myself nodding instead. Maybe I could stay for a little while longer, just until we'd heard whether his release on parole had been granted, if his home visits had convinced them he was ready. Living with the uncertainly of that would have been even harder than facing up to the reality once a decision was made. I'd have to find a way of getting home for New Year, even if it was just a flying visit, but suddenly the thought of being in New York for Christmas Day didn't seem unthinkable anymore.

'Just think about it.' Nan's voice broke into my thoughts. 'It doesn't have to be forever. But even if you agree to a few months and give Dottie the chance to consider selling the shop if you don't want to run it, I think it would make all the difference to her, and even more to you.'

'I promise I'll think about it.'

'Good and on the assumption that you'd see sense' – Nan winked – 'I shipped your Christmas presents over to Dottie. There's something else in the package that you might want to see and I got a message to say that my parcel had been delivered, so she should be able to give it to you the next time you see her.'

Nan was three steps ahead of me every time and all I could do was smile. Luckily, I'd at least had the foresight to buy and wrap my grandparents' gifts before I'd left for New York. 'Thank you and, if I don't speak to you again beforehand, I want you to have the best holiday ever.' I blew Nan a kiss. 'I love you, and please tell Granddad how much I love and miss him too.'

'I will darling, and we both love you more than you'll ever know.'

Ending the FaceTime call, I stared at the blank screen. Like those novelty road signs that tell you how many miles it is to the North Pole, all routes suddenly seemed to be leading to New York. But I needed to speak to someone about it. Someone who'd be able to help me weigh up the pros and cons, without any real investment in my decision.

* * *

'I'm so glad you were free to meet.' The paths in Central Park had been cleared, but the snow had fallen heavily again overnight, and the grass was hidden under piles of fresh white snow. If we'd stumbled upon a village of log cabins, with elves sledging down the slopes, it wouldn't have looked out of place.

'Did you call Harry first?' Paula looked up at me, navigating the way through a patch of snow that had slid back down on to the path.

'No. I thought talking to him would just muddy the waters.' I swallowed – she was his best friend, but she was also a psychotherapist, so it probably wasn't worth me trying to hide anything from her anyway. 'I can't think straight when he's around. Sorry, that sounds like a bad pick-up line, but it's true. And I *really* need to think straight about this.'

'He feels the same about you, you know.' Paula pulled a face. 'Sorry, that probably isn't helping much either, but I've never seen him like this about anyone before.'

'If things were straightforward, I'd be certain that staying in New York was the right thing to do. But I'm just not sure.'

'What? About the offer your aunt made you to take over the shop?'

'I love working in the shop, spending time with Harry, and having a whole group of new friends. It's given me the sort of life over here that I could have only dreamt about back home. But I don't deserve any of it.'

'Because of what happened to your parents?' Paula's eyes clouded as I bit my lip. We'd talked about it a bit before, but as she'd told me at the beginning, the art classes weren't really therapy sessions. There was a bit of group therapy involved in the analysis of some of the paintings, but they were more just an outlet for releasing feelings, and for my new group of friends, another excuse to get together. I'd told Paula about my aunt's offer and she knew the basic story of the accident, but we hadn't explored it in depth. I'd never talked to her about how much I felt I'd left them down, by not fighting hard enough to ensure Grant Bailey's conviction reflected his crimes. Or how guilty I felt about the prospect of leaving them in the churchyard and starting a new life thousands of miles away, too. A bird flew across our path and perched on one of the branches of a tree to the left of us, all by itself, which seemed somehow symbolic. I just hoped Paula could say something that might help.

'There's so much I think I could have done differently.' I paused for a moment, but I had to get all of this out there. 'I could have booked different flights that wouldn't have put them on the road in the dark, when it was still icy. I could have driven them myself and maybe that would have changed the outcome. Most of all I could have kept fighting to make sure that the man who caused the accident understood just how devastating his actions were. It feels as if he's walked away from this with barely any consequences to him.'

'I'm sure you've been told a hundred times already that the accident wasn't your fault and that you did everything you could to make sure you got justice for your parents?' Paula looked up at me again.

'More like a thousand.'

'And none of that makes a difference, right?'

'Right.'

'And what do you think your mom would say to you, if you could ask her what to do?'

'She'd tell me to do whatever makes me happy. She always did.' I hugged my arms to my body, the familiar catch in the back of my throat making my voice raspy.

'And your dad?'

'He'd tell me Harry was a keeper. He was never that keen on my boyfriends, but I just have this feeling I can't explain, that both of my parents would have loved Harry.'

'And is Harry the only reason you'd be staying in New York, if you decided to accept your aunt's offer?' Paula didn't take her eyes off mine.

'No, he's a big part of it, but I've never enjoyed a job more than I enjoy working in the shop, and I want to help raise funds for the Community Center. I feel like I've made new friends already, and the city just feels like home. I don't want to leave Aunt Dottie to have to find someone to run the shop either, if she's serious about giving up work.'

'So why do you want to go home?'

'For my grandparents.'

'And?' Nothing much got past Paula.

'And to punish myself for what happened to my parents when there's things I could have done differently. But most of all because I don't want to let them down again, by leaving them all alone, buried in the ground, halfway around the world. I wasn't there for them when they needed me most and I've got to try to make up for that.'

'I'm not even going to try to tell you that none of this is down to you, because I know you still aren't ready to hear it. But if you think it's all your fault, then why do you hate the guy who was driving the other car so much?'

'Because it was his fault too.'

'And did you do something you *knew* would be putting your parents in the path of danger?'

'No, I was just trying to save some money on the flights.' My voice caught again. I hated myself every time I said those words out loud.

'Like most normal people do every day, then?' Paula gave me another one of her intense looks – if she'd asked me to hand over my pin number and all my passwords, at that stage, I think I'd have been powerless to refuse. 'And what about the guy who drove the other car? Did he do something he knew presented a high risk of hurting other people?'

'Yes, but...'

'No buts! What he did isn't what normal people do. That isn't what everyone does, every day. It was the action of a selfish, thoughtless person, who you could argue *doesn't* deserve anything good in their lives. But that's not you, Libby. Far from it.'

'They're talking about letting him out of prison. He's already having home visits and his family only live a few streets away from my grandparents.' The tears I'd desperately hidden from Nan filled my eyes.

'All the more reason to stay here.' Paula suddenly sounded less like a therapist, and more like a friend.

'But my grandparents are there.'

'And what do they want you to do?'

'They want me to stay in New York.'

'Well, you either need to change your deodorant then, or you need to start listening to them. *And* to yourself.'

'My parents are back there too. The churchyard where their ashes are buried is just around the corner from my grandparents' place.' I know it probably sounded crazy, but the thought of just leaving them there made me shiver in a way that had nothing to do with the cold.

'Do you think that's where your parents really are? Because I think they're in here.' Paula put her hand over her heart. 'And if you really listen, I think you'll find they're adding their voices to the chorus telling you to stay too.'

I nodded. 'Thank you, Paula. I will think about it, I promise.' It was the second promise I'd made in as many hours, and I meant it. I would think about it. But whatever decision I made, it wasn't going to be easy.

Paula swerved around another lump of snow that had fallen on to the path, lightening the mood. 'I think we need to get Madison's firemen down here to clear the paths again.'

'Purely for health and safety reasons of course.'

'Absolutely.' Paula laughed. 'Although if I could persuade DeShawn to borrow one of their uniforms...'

I smiled back at her. 'You two look great together.'

'If a client told me that they were thinking about doing what DeShawn and I are thinking about doing, I'd tell them they needed a course of therapy to get their head straight.'

'Do I want to know what you're thinking of doing?' I was already dealing with Aunt Dottie's regular updates about her couple's massage sessions with Brian, so I really wasn't sure I wanted to hear about anyone else's private lives – especially if it involved them wearing uniforms.

'Nothing kinky, don't worry!' She laughed again. 'But he's asked me to marry him, and we've been going out for less than a month.'

'Okay... I suppose that does *sound* rushed. But you've known each other quite a while, haven't you?'

'Two years.'

'See, now that seems perfectly respectable, and if *you* think it's the right thing to do, who cares what other people think? There are no guarantees in life, anyway. You could date for five years, but would it make a difference?'

'Who's supposed to be the therapist here?' Paula had a thoughtful look on her face. 'But you're right, there are no guarantees. And that's why none of us can get through life without taking some risks. How about I will, if you will? If you stay in New York, I'll say yes to DeShawn, and if you leave, I might just make him wait those five years.'

'Do you blackmail all your clients?'

'You're not a client, you're a friend. But, yeah, I'm not averse to a bit of blackmail if I run out of other ideas.' She laughed. 'So, is it a deal?'

'If you're prepared to risk turning someone like DeShawn

down, then I can risk weighing up my options.' I stuck out my hand. 'It's a deal.'

I didn't really believe that Paula would turn him down if I decided to leave, but she'd given me a lot to think about. And the fact that she cared enough to make the deal – even if she wouldn't be able to stick to it – meant a lot. Picking up the pace as the snow began to fall again, I followed her out of the park and past Grace and Charlie's bench, saying a silent hello to them. Even they'd be hard to say goodbye to. New York might have been doing a great job of mending my heart, but it was stealing it a piece at a time too.

11

I felt like a teenager, sneaking back into the house with my shoes in my hand as we took the long way back to Candy Cane Lane after breakfast. Harry had taken me out for pancakes, and it was almost as if we were cheating on Dannie and Rob by not having breakfast at the deli. But we were still trying to keep our relationship a bit less of a talking point than DeShawn and Paula had managed. I was pretty sure that Harry had confided in her how much time we were spending together, and everyone knew we were dating. But if I told Dannie just how often we were together, he'd start mentioning wedding bells again, and Aunt Dottie would be putting both of our names on the deeds to the shop.

'So you still haven't been up to the top of the Empire State Building yet?' Harry slipped his arm around my waist and, for once, I wasn't looking forward to going to the shop. The windows on the advent calendars that Madison had insisted on buying us all, were opening far too fast. I'd miss the shop, but I'd miss Harry even more, and I'd rather have spent the time with him if I could.

'No, not yet. I did the Top of the Rock and the Statue of Liberty, with my aunt and Brian.' The memory of them kissing like teenagers, on the boat out to Liberty Island, made me laugh. I couldn't go home without seeing my namesake again, though. She was one of the few sights I'd made time for on my business trips, too. But, somehow, I still hadn't managed to fit in that longed-for trip to the top of the Empire State Building.

'I think we should put that right. In fact, I've got two tickets to the observation deck for Christmas Eve.'

'What time?'

'Seven o'clock. It's so much more spectacular when it's dark.' He held my gaze, both of us knowing this was a risk, but for very different reasons. He'd taken a chance and booked the tickets, in the hope they might tip the balance to persuade me stay. But the truth was, he'd been more than enough for me to want to do that all along; now I just had to decide whether to take the risk of following my heart.

'I should be on my way to the airport by then.'

'*Should* be?' Harry turned me to face him and I nodded. 'But it's not definite any more?'

'I've been thinking about the offer my aunt made me to run the shop, at least for a little while.' Saying it out loud, it seemed more real than ever. After my conversation with Paula, it had felt like a possibility. But now it felt like more of a probability. I didn't want to make Harry any promises, though, until I was sure. 'Nothing's certain yet, so don't waste the ticket on me.'

'Just the fact that you're thinking about it, is like Christmas come early for me.' Harry kissed me, right there, standing in the middle of the sidewalk, and a tour bus driving past honked its horn. At least we were entertaining the tourists.

'I meant what I said.' Even as I spoke, I wasn't sure I really did mean it any more. Before I'd spoken to Paula, staying would only have been about following my heart, but now it felt as if my head was saying the same thing. Being in New York made sense too.

Maybe not forever, but at least until my grandparents were home and we knew whether Grant Bailey was planning to stick around once he had the choice about where to live. But I still didn't want Harry to change his plans for me. He was supposed to be going home to see his family and I knew better than anyone how important it was to do that at Christmas. You never knew when it might be the last time. 'Don't save the ticket for me, just in case I'm not here.'

'I don't want to take anyone else, so I'm prepared to risk it.'

'What about your nephews and the rest of your family? You could go home and see them. My aunt's in Barbados for Christmas, but, if I stay, I'm sure I can gate crash Dannie and Rob's plans. If you've got the chance, you should be with your family, and you'll never get there in time if you're still here on Christmas Eve.'

'When I said I wasn't sure I could make it, my sister could barely hide her relief!' Harry laughed. 'My brother-in-law was offered the use of a house with its own pool in Florida, by one of his clients. It's all a bit last minute, but the kids have always wanted to do the whole Disney thing and my parents said they'd pay for the flights for everyone for Christmas. The problem is, it's only got three bedrooms, so if I'd wanted to go, it would have meant moving everyone around just for a couple of nights. Or me camping out on the couch and being in everyone's way. Paula and DeShawn have invited me to spend Christmas Day with them, but if you do stay, maybe we could have our own little celebration.'

'That does sound good, but you know what I'm going to say.'

'That nothing's certain yet?' He laughed again. 'Like I said, I'm willing to take my chances. I'm just really happy it's even a possibility.'

'If I'm in New York for Christmas, there's no one I'd rather spend it with.' That was as much as I could promise, and he probably had no idea how big of a deal it was for me to be able to say that to him. I'd locked my feelings inside for so long and getting close to someone new came with the biggest risk of all, but Harry had somehow got past all of that.

'That's good enough for me.' He let go of my hand as we got to the door of Candy Cane Lane. 'I'll see you at the art jam tomorrow, then?'

'I can't wait to see what you all create. But I've decided I'm just going to help Dannie and Rob with the food, seeing as people will probably offer to pay me not to produce any artwork!' Despite attending all of Paula's art classes, my drawings still looked like the ones that the parents of a five-year-old would discreetly slip into the recycling bin, when their little darling wasn't watching.

'I'm sure they'll be glad of your help.' Even Harry, as lovely as he was, couldn't argue about my lack of artistic talent. 'I'm sorry that I can't see you tonight, but I've got to work.'

'It's okay, I've promised to help Dannie and Rob with some of the food prep anyway. Are you doing more tours tonight?'

'I've got one straight after work, and then a few other bits I need to do after that.'

'I'll see you tomorrow then.' Glancing over my shoulder, to make sure Dannie wasn't there waving a box of confetti, I kissed him again. I really could spend Christmas Eve at the top of the Empire State Building with Harry, if I chose to, and right then I couldn't think of anything I wanted more.

* * *

'Valentine's day decorations already?' I unpacked the latest delivery to Candy Cane Lane and looked across at Madison, who was wearing reindeer antlers and a permanent dreamy smile on her face.

'Let's have a look.' She almost pushed me out of the way to get to the box, which was filled with strings of hand carved wooden hearts. 'I might actually have the sort of man in my life who'll buy me flowers for Valentine's Day next year.'

'I take it things are still going well?'

'Better than I ever thought possible. He calls me when he says he will, and turns up on time for our dates.'

'That's definitely a good start.' I smiled, but I hoped Madison wasn't rushing into things again. I wasn't going to offer her any advice, though. I felt even less qualified to do that than I had when I'd arrived in New York.

'Hello girls, what do you think of the hair?' Aunt Dottie walked through the shop door and pointed to her head. How her hair hadn't fallen out years ago, I'd never know. There were four strips of red, interspersed with strips of peroxide blonde, so that it looked almost white – like a candy cane. My great aunt never did anything by halves.

'I think that's above and beyond commitment to the shop!' I had to smile; there was no way Dottie would ever blend into a crowd. 'It's amazing.'

'Is it a wig?' Madison screwed up her face as if she'd smelt something terrible. She clearly wasn't a fan.

'Of course not. Some of us are just prepared to go the distance.' Dottie laughed, not seeming in the least bit offended. 'Do you mind taking your lunch break now, Madison? There's something I need to talk to Libby about.'

'You're not gonna get rid of me, are you? I think your hair looks great.' Madison widened her eyes, like people do when they're lying – or panicking. I was pretty sure she was doing both.

'Of course not, there's just some family business we need to discuss.' Aunt Dottie was already waving her out of the shop. Whether she wanted her lunch break or not, she was going to be taking it.

'So, what was it you wanted to talk about?' By the time I'd got back from the deli, with Dottie's requested cinnamon and pumpkin spiced latte, and a frosted doughnut, she was sitting behind the counter. I had a pretty good idea what she wanted to say, but you never quite knew with her. She could be about to tell me that she and Brian had decided to get matching tattoos, and to ask my advice on the best place to put them. Anything was possible with Dottie and it was one of the things I loved most about her.

'I just want to talk some sense into you.'

'Is this about the shop?' I set the coffee and doughnut down on the counter next to her. 'I am thinking about it, I promise. I'll give you an answer by the end of the week, and Madison has already said she'll cover extra shifts if I decide to leave. At least until you can get someone else in.'

'It's not about the shop, it's about you.'

'What have I done?' I hated the thought that I might have done something to disappoint her and she had an uncharacteristically serious expression on her face.

'It's what you're about to do that's worrying me. If you leave New York, you're gonna regret it for the rest of your life.'

'It's great here, but—'

'I'm not talking about the place, I'm talking about giving up on making a new life for yourself.' Dottie tore a piece off from her doughnut. 'I should know, I did it myself when I came here. Running away is never the answer.'

'I'm not following. You want me to stay in New York, but you think you made a mistake by coming here?'

'I said I'd tell you how I ended up here one day and today's that day. Put the closed sign up on the door; it's time you had a chance to learn from my mistakes before you make a huge one of your own.'

'But it's a week before Christmas. If we close up now we could be throwing money away.' My objection was wasted. It was obvious, from the look on her face, that she wasn't going to change her mind, so I turned the sign around and slid the bolt across.

'What do you know about why my marriage broke up?' She fixed me with a look that wouldn't have been out of place on an interrogator.

'Not a lot. Just that it didn't end well.'

'It didn't end well because I had an affair.' Dottie shook her head. 'I'm not proud of it, and it broke my husband's heart.'

'People make mistakes.'

'Yes, they do.' She gave me that same look again. 'But some mistakes are more deliberate than others. I hurt Colin, and I've been paying for it ever since, even though I didn't have to.'

'Aren't you happy here?'

'I am now, but it's taken a long time, and it's only since Brian that I've stopped wanting to turn the clock back.' I held my breath, hoping she wasn't about to launch into another description of Brian's healing hands. 'You see, Colin offered to take me back after the affair, and I really wanted to. It was only when he found out about the other man that I realised how much I loved him.'

'So, what happened?' Despite the fact she was almost eighty, it wasn't hard to picture two men fighting over my great aunt. She was what the phrase *a force of nature* had been created for. What was much harder to imagine was my aunt ever choosing to do something that made her unhappy. She'd always seemed uncompromising in her belief that life was what you made it, and this was a whole new side to her.

'What happened is that I couldn't forgive *myself*, even though Colin was more than willing to. So I left him, and I left Canterbury and came here. I missed him every day, and in some ways, I still do, even though he's been dead for nearly six years. I punished myself for more than twenty, but meeting Brian made me realise I couldn't do that any more. I didn't *want* to do it any more. I can't stand the idea of it taking you twenty years, Lib. You've wasted enough time already, and what happened wasn't your fault.'

'I had no idea about you and Colin.'

'And I wouldn't have mentioned it, except I thought it might make a difference, and I want you to stay.' She held up her hand. 'But before you say anything, it's got nothing to do with wanting you to run the shop. Work here, or don't work here. You can become a nightclub waitress, or join a Broadway chorus line for all I care, just stay and live your life, Lib.'

'Have you been talking to Nan?' I already knew the answer to that.

'Of course I have, and they want you to stay too. You know they only keep that goddamn pub open for your benefit, don't you?'

I shook my head. That couldn't be true. 'But Granddad loves it.' I couldn't bear the thought that I'd been holding them back all this time, rather than helping them out.

'Yeah, and he loves you more. Come on Libby, you know we're right. It's time to move on. Don't make the same mistakes I did.' As Aunt Dottie stuffed the rest of the doughnut into her mouth, I just nodded. She could be blunt, but she was right. I probably was stopping my grandparents from moving on.

'I am starting to accept that I'll never know if there's anything I could have done to change what happened and that the accident wasn't my fault.' I'd never have dreamt I could say that and really believe it, but I did.

'And what about what happened afterwards, with the court case for that worthless piece of—' Aunt Dottie didn't finish the sentence, but she didn't have to. I knew exactly what she thought of Grant Bailey and it was spot on.

'That's a bit more difficult to accept. I still feel like I could have done more.'

'Not according to your grandparents.' Dottie shook her head. 'You weren't the judge and you didn't write the laws. None of it is your fault. But even if all of it was down to you, making decisions for the future, because you want to punish yourself for the past, might be the dumbest idea I've ever heard.'

'That's what I like about you.' I couldn't help laughing. 'You always give it to me straight.'

'I'm a little old lady.' Dottie shrugged, knowing the description had never suited anyone less. 'And if I can't say it straight, who else is gonna?'

'Thank you.' I squeezed her hand. She'd given me a lot to think about, but she clearly wasn't done yet.

'I've got the package Ruby sent over for you and I'll get Brian to drop it off when he comes to pick me up.' Dottie ran a hand through her stripey hair. 'Don't you think the fact she went to all that trouble tells you everything you need to know about what she wants you to do?'

All I could do was nod in response. I'd spent so long telling myself that my grandparents needed me, when it was me who'd needed to hide myself away in their world. I had to give them the space to work out their next steps, as much as I had to decide on mine, and the reasons for leaving New York were fast disappearing.

12

I saw the huge piece of street art, on the wall that was causing all the problems, from the end of the street.

'Wow, did one of you guys paint this?' I stood next to DeShawn, who shook his head.

'I wish.'

'We think it's a Parsy! Isn't it great?' Abbie said as she came over with Karly. George and Olly – Karly's pugs – were trotting behind.

'It definitely looks the same style as the one under the arch in Central Park.' It was like a depiction of the last supper, but everyone sitting around the table represented someone who used the Community Center, from lone parents, holding sleeping children, to elderly people, and even someone holding a paintbrush. I didn't recognise any of the faces, but it captured perfectly what the place was about. If Parsy was just an anonymous artist, somehow he'd got the inside track.

'He usually tweets a picture, if it's one of his, and claims responsibility for it.' Abbie glanced down at her phone for about the tenth time since we'd started talking. 'If he does, it might be enough to save the Community Center on its own.'

'I'm really trying not to pin all my hopes on this. But, if it is confirmed as a Parsy, we'd be able to auction the wall off. Which means not only could we make the area safe, and get the electrics done, but we might even be able to extend the building into this space.' Karly couldn't stop smiling, and I was already desperate to get my phone out and start checking Twitter too.

'You're right, let's try not to get ahead of ourselves, until we know for sure.' Paula was the voice of reason, but I so wanted Karly to be right. I just hoped it wasn't all too good to be true.

'What's going on? What are we missing?' Dannie walked up behind us, followed by Rob and Harry. They were wheeling the street food cart that Rob had borrowed from a friend, who, according to Dannie, usually ran it down by Battery Park, but was away visiting family for the holidays.

'We think it might be a Parsy.' Karly was grinning again.

'But how?' Rob looked at his sister. 'How did no one see him do it?'

'I don't know. But, if it really is his, it could save this place.' Karly picked up one of the pugs. 'What do you think, Olly, is it the real deal?'

'Oh my God! It is, it is, it's one of his!' For a moment I actually thought the pug had gained the power of speech, but then I nearly got knocked off my feet by Abbie, who was running around high fiving everyone in turn. 'It's just come up on his Twitter feed, it's definitely a Parsy!'

'It's such good news, isn't it?' I finally managed to speak to Harry when then celebrations started to die down. It still seemed almost impossible to believe that a Parsy had appeared on the wall overnight. But it was there in front of us and the more I looked at it, the more beautiful I realised it was.

'It is. I'm so pleased for Karly, and everyone else who relies on the Community Center.' He smiled, but there were dark circles under his eyes.

'So how did it go last night?' I waited for an answer, and he looked at me blankly for a moment. 'The tour, and the other stuff you had to do?'

'It was good. I got a great tip from the family I showed around. Although it's like small change compared to a Parsy.' He smiled again, taking my hand in his and giving it a squeeze. I noticed there were flecks of different coloured paint on his sleeve. He saw me looking and added, 'And the other stuff was for the book. I don't want to tell everyone else yet, but I've had some interest from one of the agents I approached. They think they can find a publisher for it, but they want to see some more illustrations first, so I spent a lot of last night doing those.'

'That's great.' I put my arms around his neck, all the good news making me forget about keeping things low key in front of the others.

'Much as I hate to interrupt this, I need to borrow Libby to help set up the stall. Abbie's just retweeted the Parsy, and told the whole world about the art jam, so we better get ready to serve the world too.' Dannie virtually dragged me away from Harry, pushing him in DeShawn's direction at the same time. 'Well, chicken, you kept quiet about how serious you two have been getting!'

'I wouldn't say serious.' I tried my best to look casual, but I had a horrible feeling I had the same sort of look on my face that Madison had been wearing for the last couple of weeks.

'Whatever you say, Lib.' Dannie winked, clearly not buying a word of it, and I couldn't say I blamed him. I wasn't buying a word of it myself any more, either.

'So, what do you think about this Parsy, then?' I hadn't really expected the change of subject to work, but it seemed that a piece of street art by Parsy was even more exciting for Dannie than discussing my love life.

'I know, we were just saying that we think it might be someone we know. Weren't we, Rob?'

'Uh-huh.' Rob looked up from turning the skewers of chicken over on the grill. 'And I think you know who it is too.'

'I do?' I frowned, wondering who they could be referring to.

'DeShawn!' Dannie said his name in the loudest whisper I'd ever heard and, when DeShawn looked around as a result, he ducked down behind the cart. If it was possible to shout a whisper, then Dannie had just done it.

'Get up, you're making him look over.' Rob laughed. 'At least I know you'll never be able to have a secret affair; you're useless at being discreet.'

'Do you really think it's him?' I looked over at Paula's boyfriend, as Dannie stood up again. 'His paintings up in the studio are great, but then there must be thousands of talented artists in Manhattan. What makes you so sure it's him?'

'It can't be a coincidence that the Community Center needs saving, and then, all of sudden, a Parsy appears on the wall, can it?' Rob tapped the side of his forehead, and I couldn't help agreeing.

'And his name's DeShawn *Parshall* – Parsy. See, it really does makes sense when you think about it,' Dannie said. 'Go on, admit it, it does make sense, doesn't it?'

I looked across at DeShawn again, as he laughed at something Paula said. 'It's plausible, and I think you're right. Parsy has got to be someone who knows this place.' I had to admit he looked the part too; he could have passed for a rap star, so why not New York's most famous street artist? But now Dannie had put the idea in my head that it could be someone we knew, my mind couldn't help flashing to the dark circles under Harry's eyes and the flecks of paint on his sleeve. I had the strangest of feelings that there was something he wasn't telling me about what he'd been up to the night before.

* * *

'Thank you all again so much for today. To friendship!' Karly held up her glass as we sat in Rob and Dannie's deli, after what had turned out to be a long but fantastic day. It was at least the fourth toast Karly had made, and she was starting to slur her words a bit, as Rob put an arm around her.

'Before my sister actually slides under the table, maybe someone else can lead the next toast?'

'I've got something to toast actually.' I looked around the table, just hoping they were going to be as pleased to hear the news as I was to share it, now that I'd finally made a decision. 'Here's to living in New York.'

'We're already living in New York.' Karly raised her glass anyway, and then started giggling.

'Does this mean what I think it does, chicken?' Dannie grabbed hold of my wrist. 'Please tell me I'm right.'

'You are. I've decided to stay on. I'm not sure exactly how long for, yet, but I'm not making any plans to leave.'

'That's fantastic! And there I was thinking this day couldn't get any better.' Dannie kissed me on the cheek, spilling half of his champagne down me. It was like Abbie confirming that the artwork was a Parsy all over again, with everyone hugging and chinking their glasses together.

Harry was the last person to speak to me. 'You're really staying?'

'For as long as I can.' It was all I could promise, but it seemed to be enough for him.

'I don't know what changed your mind, but whatever it was,

I'm really glad it happened.' Harry kissed me, and a big cheer went up from around the table. There was no point even trying to convince Dannie that dating Harry was a casual thing now, and I was past caring.

'We need to celebrate. We're all young, well *young-ish*.' Dannie looked at Rob and laughed. 'We should go to *Copacabana* or *Le Bain*.'

'Maybe some other time. I think we're going to hit the sack early tonight.' Paula looked at DeShawn who nodded in response. I'd seen him stifling yawns the whole time we'd been in the deli. If he'd been up all night putting the artwork on the wall, I was surprised he could even keep his eyes open.

'I could use an early night too. I really want to celebrate you staying, but I'm not sure I can handle clubbing.' Harry's eyes met mine, and I could have kissed him again. Maybe I should have been spending my time in New York trying out as many of the bars and clubs as I could, but I wouldn't swap any of that for a night with my friends from the Community Center, and I definitely wouldn't swap it for a night with Harry.

'I'm with you. I've got to open the shop tomorrow, and Dottie will hang me from one of the trees in Central Park if I'm late doing that four days before Christmas.'

'Looks like it's just us then. Are you guys up for it?' Dannie turned to Karly and Abbie, who both nodded, and within minutes we were out on the street. Paula and DeShawn set off for her apartment, and the others headed off to the club, leaving Harry and me outside Candy Cane Lane.

'Back to mine, then?' Harry's smile melted away as I shook my head.

'No, let's go to my place.' I put my hand on his face. 'If I'm going to stay, I might as well start treating the apartment like I actually live there. Especially as Aunt Dottie has made the move to

Brian's place permanent. There's no point it sitting empty, is there?'

'None at all.' Harry kissed me, and the snow that had held off all day for the art jam, started to fall silently onto the sidewalk. I couldn't imagine wanting to ever spend Christmas anywhere else – but things could change as quickly as the New York weather.

13

Christmas Eve morning was much busier in the shop than I'd thought it would be. I'd assumed everyone would have decorated their trees by that point, and that the call for Christmas ornaments would be over. But I hadn't realised how many people bought them as gifts, and there was a lot of last-minute shopping going on. Dannie had been over the moon to be picked out as the winner of the Swarovski bauble, but it wasn't that big of a surprise, considering he must have bought about 80 per cent of the tickets. Betty had the day off to spend with her family, and Aunt Dottie had already set off for Barbados with Brian for a week. She said she wanted to feel the sun on her skin, but I'd zoned out when she started talking about a natural saltwater spa, that was most effective if you bathed naked. It wasn't the image of Christmas I wanted to keep in my head.

I'd agreed to go with Harry to the top of the Empire State Building after I closed up the shop for the day and Madison had headed off to see her fireman. Then we were going to meet the others at the Community Center, before spending Christmas Day at the deli. Rob had offered to cook for all of us, and I hadn't needed much persuading. He was making Italian chicken and roast pork belly, so it wouldn't be a traditional Christmas dinner, like the ones I'd had with my parents. It made it easier to accept, somehow, that I was celebrating Christmas at all without them there.

I was almost ready to close up the shop when the bell jangled, and a woman came in pushing another older lady in a wheelchair. I looked up and smiled, almost certain it was the bride I'd seen at the Rockefeller Center, the day Harry had shown me a New York Christmas.

'I thought you'd be closed.' She had a dusting of snow on her coat, which fell on to the shop floor as she bent down to tuck the blanket around the other woman's legs.

'I was just about to close up, but you're more than welcome to look around. I don't need to get away for twenty minutes or so.' I'd sent Madison home half an hour early, because she'd been desperate to get ready for the party at the firehouse, and apparently no less than three hours would do. The customers had finally tailed off by that point, and I'd been tidying up and enjoying a bit of time to think about Mum and Dad. I tried to focus on the good times – the wonderful Christmas Eves *we had* shared – and not the fact that there would never be another one. I was getting better at it all the time. At least I'd thought I was.

'Thanks so much. We've been meaning to come in here for three weeks, but we just haven't been able to get around to it. We didn't want to go home to Rock Springs without getting something for the tree next year, though. Did we, Mom?'

'That's right, honey.'

'You've been visiting for three weeks?' I looked at the younger woman again, not sure if I should say anything about the wedding, just in case it wasn't her.

'That's right. Are you British?' She smiled as I nodded. 'I've always wanted to go to London. Is it true that you can tell if the King's at home when he's flying the flag over Buckingham Palace?'

'I think so.' I laughed. I'd never been quite sure if that was true or not, but her eyes lit up all the same.

'Oh I always love meeting Brits, you've got the best accent! I'm Jessica' – she stuck out her hand – 'and this is my mom, Blanche.'

'Great to meet you both. I'm Libby.'

'See this one?' Blanche looked up at me as she spoke, and I nodded. 'Jessie should be in Europe on her honeymoon right now.'

'Mom, don't.'

'I'm sorry...' Thank God I hadn't mentioned the wedding. If it was her at the Rockefeller Center, and the groom had already skipped out, then the last thing she needed was me mentioning the photos.

'Don't be, we're having a wonderful time here.' She didn't look like a woman who'd been run out on. 'Brad and I were originally planning to have a honeymoon in Europe, but Mom and Dad have never had the chance to visit New York before, so we decided to have the wedding here instead. Brad booked an adapted apartment on the Upper East Side, and I wouldn't swap it for Europe. In fact, I wouldn't have swapped these last three weeks for the world.'

Her mother reached up and laid her hand on Jessica's. Her bones were visible through the skin, and I knew instantly why her daughter wouldn't have swapped the time they had together for anything.

'You know what? I think I saw you at the Rockefeller Center, having your wedding photos taken.'

'Really?' Jessica's eyes lit up. 'I thought I was going to be real shy when it came to it, having the photos taken like that in front of everyone. But I couldn't get enough of it. I wanted to capture every moment with Brad, and Mom and Dad.' Jessica laughed. 'The photographer almost had to lasso me, to get me out of there.'

'You looked amazing. All of you.' They exchanged a smile.

As painful as it would have been, I wished I'd known that the last time I saw my parents would be the last time. I had so much still to tell them, and now I never could. I knew it must have been really tough losing someone slowly, too, like Jessica was losing her mum. But they'd been given the chance to do things together – to say goodbye properly, to make memories, and capture them in a thousand photographs. I envied them that. 'So, is there something in particular that you're looking for, for your tree?'

'It doesn't necessarily have to be a tree decoration, we just want something to remind us of the trip.'

'What about this?' I took the last snow globe down from the shelf. The tree inside was decorated almost exactly like the one at the Rockefeller Center, and when I handed it to Jessica, it was obvious she saw the resemblance too.

'It's perfect. Don't you think, Mom?'

'It is, honey, just like every moment of this trip.' Jessica handed over her credit card, but I shook my head.

'Please, take it, it's a gift.'

'Oh, no, I couldn't...' Jessica shook her head, still holding out her card.

'Please, it would mean a lot to me.' I couldn't buy my parents a Christmas present any more, but I could do this.

'Thank you so much.' Jessica slid the credit card back inside her purse and squeezed my hand. 'Merry Christmas.'

'Merry Christmas to you, too.'

'Oh shoot!' Jessica looked at her watch and widened her eyes. 'I promised Brad I'd pick a pie up from the deli and they're about to close. I know you are too, but if I run, could I leave Mom to look at the decorations? I'm getting better at manoeuvring the chair, but the snow's starting up again and it's so lovely in here. I promise I'll be real quick.'

She looked embarrassed at having to ask and guilty at needing to leave her mum, even for a few minutes, but I knew how busy it would be outside with last-minute shoppers crowding the side-walk. 'Of course! It'll be nice to have the company while I close up.'

'That's right.' Blanche smiled. 'And no one should be alone on Christmas Eve.'

'Thanks so much.' Jessica was out of the door in a flash, but her mother's words had hit me unexpectedly, and an image of the churchyard back in Canterbury suddenly flitted into my mind. *No one should be alone on Christmas Eve.* The guilt that had plagued me for so long, felt as if it was creeping up my spine. I just had to shake it off, focus on all the good memories, and the here and now. Christmas Eve was one of those days that was bound to be extra tough, when you missed someone the way I missed Mum and Dad.

'It was so kind of you to give Jessie the snow globe.' Blanche had such a kind face and, despite her obvious frailty, her eyes lit up every time she smiled.

'It was an absolute pleasure. I think they're the best thing we sell in the shop.'

'I reckon you might be right, and I know she'll be thinking of me every time she looks at it, when I'm not here any more.' There wasn't a hint of self-pity in Blanche's voice. 'We got to make so many memories on this trip. I know she'll be thinking of them every Christmas from now on too, and that gives me so much comfort. My pastor always says that a person dies twice. Once when their heart stops beating and once when they're forgotten. But they don't truly die at all until that second time, you see? And I know I won't really be gone all the time Jessie remembers me and does the things we used to do together.'

'I'm sure she always will.' I could have said so much more, but I was almost choking on the words. I'd been so busy focusing on the here and now that I hadn't even made arrangements to fly home for New Year, to be at my grandparents' party, or to be with Mum and Dad for our New Year's Day tradition. They might have told me to stay on in New York, but I had no idea how many more years I'd have with Nan and Granddad, and I didn't want to miss the chance to make a single memory. I could tell myself that Christmas Eve was just making me maudlin and, despite Blanche's words, not being with my parents over Christmas didn't feel nearly as much of a betrayal as missing out on our tradition of spending New Year's Day together. I needed to call the airline before I even thought about going to meet Harry.

By the time Jessica came hurtling back through the door less than five minutes after she'd left, I'd already put the call through and had my mobile on speaker phone, while I waited in the queue to speak to someone from customer service. Thankfully the on-hold music was a medley of festive songs, so I'd been able to keep chatting to Blanche and pretend it was all part of the Christmas Eve experience in Candy Cane Lane. She'd told me how she hoped to live long enough to become a grandma, and the lump that had already formed in my throat had become a boulder.

'Thank you so much for that.' Jessica hugged me like we were old friends and then Blanche took hold of my hand, as they went to leave.

'I hope you're spending the holidays with the people who mean the most to you.'

The boulder in my throat was getting bigger by the second and it was a miracle that I managed to say anything at all. 'Thank you, have a wonderful Christmas.' I pulled the bolt across the top of the shop door as soon as they left and turned to lean against it. Jessica hadn't thought twice about giving up her honeymoon to spend three weeks in New York with her mum and dad, but I hadn't even been able to make time to arrange a new flight to make sure I was home for New Year. I'd got completely caught up in my life in Manhattan, and it had felt so good not to be dwelling on the past for once, but I suddenly felt pulled in two directions. My new friends meant a lot to me, and most of all New York was where Harry was. But there were still four people back home who mattered just as much to me as he did, and if I couldn't get home for New Year, I'd be letting them all down.

'Good afternoon, this is Jenna speaking. How may I be of assistance?' As I finally reached the front of the queue for the airline call centre, I snatched up my phone.

'Oh hi, I was supposed to be on a flight out of JFK to Heathrow tonight, but I was wondering if I could change my flight for some time after Christmas, but before New Year's Eve.'

'I'm really sorry, but it's too late to transfer a flight scheduled for today.'

'Of course, that's fine.' I didn't care about losing the money for my original flight. All I wanted was to make sure I could get home in time for New Year. 'It doesn't matter about transferring it, but can I book a new one to get home in time for the thirty-first?'

'Let me just check that for you. Is it just the one seat?'

'Uh-huh.'

'Okay great, I'll just put you back on hold for a few moments.' The festive tunes filled the silence, and it felt like I was holding my breath as I waited for Jenna to come back on the line. 'I'm so sorry we don't have any guaranteed seats available until January second. You can try other airlines, but as we have the most flights on that route it's very unlikely you'll find a seat. You can come to the airport and try to get a seat on standby, if someone else cancels at the last minute. It's usually okay if you're just looking for a single seat, but we still can't guarantee it.'

'So, there's no way of making sure I'll definitely get a flight home in time for New Year?' I knew it was busy in the holidays and that there were fewer flights scheduled, but I'd been so certain I could still get home.

'Like I say, there's a good chance you'll get a standby seat, but the only way to guarantee getting home before New Year is to take your scheduled flight tonight.'

As I ended the call, I couldn't blink back the tears any longer. As much as I wanted to spend Christmas with Harry, Blanche's words were ringing in my ears, and I couldn't stay if it meant forgetting the most important tradition my parents and I had shared. I'd spent almost two years feeling partly responsible for them dying the first time around, and there was no way I was going to be responsible for them dying a second time, in the way Blanche had described. Catching my original flight was going to be incredibly tight, and the fact it meant I'd have no chance to explain things to Harry face to face was breaking my heart. He'd probably never forgive me for standing him up on Christmas Eve and I was going to find it really hard to forgive myself. But I knew I'd never get over standing my parents up on New Year's Day and, in the end, there was really only one choice.

* * *

There wasn't going to be any romantic trip up the Empire State Building, and I wasn't the only one who couldn't believe what I was choosing to give up.

'You're joking, right?' I could imagine the look on Paula's face just from the tone of her voice. 'You want me to tell Harry you aren't meeting him tonight, and that you'll be on a flight to London instead?'

'I know it's a lot to ask. But I want to make him understand that it isn't him, it's me, and I don't think he'll be able to hear it if I say it.'

'That's the world's worst cliché, don't you think? It's not you, it's me.'

'Usually it is. But just this once, it's true. I love... I love everything about Harry.' I couldn't bring myself to say I loved him. Even though I was certain now that I did, despite having known him for less than two months. If I was going to say those words for the first time, I'd want to say them to him, not someone else. But now I'd probably never get the chance. 'I can't stay, though. I thought I could, but I just can't.'

'And nothing I say will make any difference, I suppose?'

'You tried, everyone did, even me. But it's no good, I can't just leave my parents behind and start a new life. I need to be where they are.' I didn't want to explain everything to Paula, and the truth was I didn't have the time. If I'd told her that why I needed to get back for New Year's Day, she'd have told me that my parents weren't really in that churchyard. And even if they were looking down on me, that they'd understand why I couldn't be there this time. I knew logically that all of that made sense, but my need to be there for my parents was something only I would probably ever understand. I could still have come back after New Year, but leaving so suddenly felt like I was burning my bridges. I couldn't spend my life flitting back between New York and Canterbury, I had to choose and, by leaving like this, it felt as if the choice was already made.

'What about your aunt, and the shop?'

'Madison and Betty are going to cover until Dottie's back, and one of Betty's daughters is going to help out too, for as long as she's needed.'

'And do you really think you'll get a flight on Christmas Eve?'

'I never cancelled my original flight.'

'That says a lot.' I could picture Paula's expression again, and I was so glad I wasn't there to see it. Hurting Harry was the worst thing about all of this, but losing the rest of my friends made it almost unbearable. 'I really think it would be better if Harry heard this first hand. From you.'

'I can't, Paula. *Please*.'

'I'll do it. But I want you to know that, in my professional *and* personal opinion, I think you're making a huge mistake.'

'Thank you – for telling Harry and for trying to help. Can I ask you one more thing?'

'What? Do you want me to break into someone's house, and steal all their kids' Christmas presents from under the tree?' Paula's tone was tight, and she had every right to be angry. She was going to cause her best friend pain, because of me.

'Don't turn down DeShawn's proposal because I'm going.'

'Sorry, but a deal's a deal. And if you can walk away from a good man, then I'm damn sure I can turn down a proposal from one.' She cut off the call and I put my phone into my bag. It was 6.45 p.m. when I locked the door to Candy Cane Lane for the last time. If I ran all the way, I could still get to the Empire State Building in time to meet Harry. But instead, I turned in the opposite direction, to try and find a cab. I was going home, but I had no idea if it would ever really feel that way again.

14

It turned out that trying to get a cab on Christmas Eve wasn't easy. But the concierge at one of the hotels where I stopped to ask told me that the Columbus Circle taxi stand, on the edge of Central Park, was my best bet. I didn't want to go near the park, but I had to make my flight. It didn't make any difference, anyway, it wasn't as if I could just forget about Harry. I could be in Central Park, or in the washing powder aisle, in the Canterbury branch of Sainsbury's – he'd still be on my mind. Even as I was walking to Columbus Circle, I kept checking my phone. I don't know what I expected to see, or even what I wanted to see. Maybe a message from Paula, telling me that Harry was okay, and that he wasn't that upset by the news that I was leaving. I'd have preferred it that way, even though I felt sick at the thought of never seeing him again, and I wasn't stupid enough to think that the full weight of my decision to leave had hit me yet.

I stood outside a *Dunkin' Donuts*, a few feet from one of the road crossings, and pulled my phone out again. Still no message. Dropping the phone back into my bag, I looked up and saw a large back car speeding down the road towards the crossing. There were a couple of young girls in the road, and it should have been safe to cross, but the car wasn't showing any signs of slowing down. I'd never been much of a runner, despite the few times I'd been out with Dannie since I'd arrived in New York, and I had no idea how I did it, but I dropped the handle of my wheelie suitcase and ran faster than I ever had before, yelling at the girls and holding my hands out in front of me to push them clear of the car. Maybe it was the adrenaline, but I didn't even realise that the car had clipped me until I hit the ground in a sitting position. Turning my head, I saw the car mount the kerb up ahead, and hit the crossing sign, knocking it almost parallel with the sidewalk, and raising the two front wheels off the ground.

'Are you okay, ma'am?' A female traffic cop was in front of me in seconds, and her colleague was already cuffing the driver of the car.

My heart was hammering in my chest, but I felt strangely calm as I replied, 'I'm fine. What about the girls?'

'They're lucky to be alive, but they're okay thanks to you. We were following him, but we couldn't stop the vehicle in time.' The police car was up ahead, half on the sidewalk and half on the road. I hadn't even heard the siren, and I shook my head, mainly to see if it hurt. I hadn't hit it – at least I didn't think I had, but it had all happened so fast. 'I don't think you should move until you've been seen by a medic.'

'No way.' It had been a bad enough day, without ending it sitting in the middle of the street, with the world watching me, while the police closed the road to stop another vehicle finishing me off. More police cars were already arriving and, if I didn't get up soon, someone was probably going to force me to stay put. The car had only clipped me, and for once having a well-covered bum had done me a favour. Thank God for Rob's cheesecakes and pecan pies, otherwise I might have sustained a lot more than bruises. Struggling to my feet, I felt dizzy, but there was no way I was sitting down in the road again.

'You can at least take my arm, ma'am.' The police officer helped me to the side of the road and a couple of the waiters came out of a restaurant on the corner, with chairs for me and the two girls who I'd unceremoniously shoved on to the sidewalk. They were both in tears, and there was another police officer comforting them. Someone had picked up my suitcase for me, and someone else brought me a coffee, as the officer sat me down. I winced when my flesh made contact with the hard seat. 'What's your name, ma'am?'

'Liberty, but everyone calls me Libby.' I don't know why I said that, but I started shivering as I did. I was so busy hoping that Paula would text me something to let me off the hook that I almost hadn't seen the girls. I wouldn't have been there for them, just like I wasn't there for my parents. 'If I hadn't put my phone away when I did, I wouldn't have got to them in time.'

'The girls were very lucky you were there, Libby. I hate to think what would have happened if you hadn't been.'

'Looks like it's almost certainly a DUI.' One of the male police officers came over to us. 'The smell of liquor was overpowering when he opened the door.'

'I knew you were going to say that.' The female officer put her arm on my shoulder. 'I was just telling Libby how lucky the girls were that she was here.'

'But I nearly wasn't, I was too busy looking at my phone over there, and it would have been my fault.' I pointed to the shop as tears started to roll down my face, and I wasn't sure why. It might have been the pain, or the shock. Or it could have been because of Mum and Dad, or Harry, or even because I was leaving New York. It was probably a combination of everything. All I knew for sure was that I couldn't stop crying. It was like that first day in the park all over again.

'Listen to me, Libby.' The officer crouched in front of me, taking hold of my hands. 'Those girls are alive because of you, and that was down to good luck. Their good luck. But even if you'd still been looking at your phone on the sidewalk, the accident wouldn't have been your fault. The only person to blame is the driver who got in his car drunk.'

I looked up and tried to focus on her face, but the tears just kept coming. Someone was running towards us, and all I could make out were two blurred shapes. For a moment I thought one of them was Harry, and relief flooded through me. But then they ran past us, straight to the girls.

I couldn't really tell what was going on, because all four of them were crying and shouting, and I still couldn't stop crying either. My tears were silent, though, and the police officer was still trying to offer me words of comfort. But I wasn't taking them in either. All I wanted was Harry; he'd find a way of making it all right – he had from the first moment we'd met in the park. But I'd ruined that too.

'Thank you so much.' Suddenly a woman flung her arms around me, lifting the front two legs of my chair off the sidewalk for a second. When they went back down, it felt like my bum was hitting the road all over again, and I made a weird noise that didn't even sound like it came from me. 'Oh God, I'm so sorry. I didn't hurt you, did I?'

'No.' It was a lie. But she was already crying, and looked even more all over the place than I felt.

'You saved my girls. When they found out their dad had booked a carriage ride in the park, they went back to the hotel to charge Kayleigh's cell phone, so she could take some pictures.' She was speaking so fast, it was hard for me to keep up with what she was saying. 'Savannah's seventeen, and Mike keeps telling me that I've got to let them have a bit more freedom, and that it would be safe for them to walk four blocks in Midtown, without me holding their hand. And then this happens. I should never have let them go by themselves.'

'It's not your fault.' The words came out of my mouth, but I still couldn't see the irony – not until the girls' mother said what she said next.

'I still can't believe you risked your life for two strangers. I'd die for them, of course I would. But for you to risk that for someone you don't even know, I can never thank you enough.' It was probably just the headlights of one of the police cars being switched on, to illuminate the road, but if someone had said the whole sky had lit up at that moment, I wouldn't have disbelieved them. I could finally see what everyone had been saying – my parents would have given up their lives to save me, in a heartbeat, but the last thing they'd have wanted was for me to give up my life for them. Especially when it wouldn't do a thing to bring them back. I didn't have to be in a churchyard three and a half thousand miles away to remember them, they were with me wherever I went. I'd never felt that way more than I had in New York, but now I was terrified that I'd slammed the door on my life here too.

'I'm just glad they're okay.' Allowing the woman to subject me to another rib-crushing hug, I stood up; the worst of the dizziness seemed to have passed. 'I'm sorry, but I've got to go.' I needed to see Harry, whether I could find a cab or not, and I'd haul my bruised behind all the way to the Community Center if I had to.

'You're not going anywhere until the medics have at least checked you out.' The police officer put her hand on my arm again. 'They're here now and, if they give you the okay, I'll drive you anywhere you want to go. But if you try to leave without getting checked out first, I'll have to arrest you.' I didn't know if she was joking, but she didn't smile, so I wasn't going to risk it.

It took nearly half an hour for me to satisfy the paramedics that I didn't have any serious injuries, and even then, I had to sign a waiver to promise I wouldn't sue them if half my bum cheeks suddenly dropped off or something. I should be so lucky. They said I was probably just badly bruised, and I agreed with them every time I sat down.

The police took my details and an initial statement, but they said they'd need me to do a full witness interview after Christmas. The girls' mother had insisted on taking my mobile number, too, even though I'd told her that the hundred or so times she'd already thanked me was more than enough. As a result, it was nearly ten o'clock by the time the police officer, whose name turned out to be Susie, dropped me off at the Community Center.

Opening the door to the café, I could have believed I'd walked into a wake instead of a Christmas Eve party.

'Libby, what the hell are you doing here?' Dannie was the first to notice me, and his eyes flashed. I'd never seen him like this before.

'I'm sorry, but I've been in an accident and all I wanted was Harry. I didn't realise...' The tears were back, and it took me what felt like hours to get the whole story out – between sobs and going off on a tangent about losing Mum and Dad, meeting the girl who'd given up her honeymoon to be with her parents, and Blanche's story about someone only really dying when they were forgotten. It sounded like gobbledygook as I was saying it, so God knows if it made any sense to the others. But, somehow, they seemed to get the gist, and by the time I finally stopped for breath, Dannie was crying too.

'I'm sorry, Lib, I just thought you'd walked out on us all, without even bothering to say goodbye.'

A fresh set of tears streamed down my face. 'I don't blame you for being angry; I handled it all so badly.'

Paula moved her wheelchair to position herself next to me. 'I wish I had better news to tell you about Harry. But he didn't take the fact that you'd left very well, and he borrowed DeShawn's car. He set off for Florida, even though I told him it was crazy, but he said he had to get out of New York.'

'I'm such an idiot.' I leant on her shoulder for a moment, wishing I'd listened the first time around. But it was too late now. It was all too late.

'Let's get you home.' Rob came over and took my hand. 'Do you think you can walk?'

'I've got my mom's car, so I'll drop you back on the way home.' Abbie smiled in my direction, and I tried to smile back, but my mouth wouldn't cooperate.

'I'm sorry.' I seemed to be saying that a lot. 'I didn't mean to break up the party.'

'It wasn't much of a party without you anyway, chicken.' Dannie took one of my arms as he spoke, and Rob supported me on the other side. I couldn't believe I'd been willing to leave all of this behind, or that they were prepared to forgive me. I'd lost Harry, though, so maybe they thought that was enough punishment for anyone.

* * *

Dannie and Rob had tried to persuade me to stay at their place, but in the end, I'd finally managed to convince them that I'd be better on my own. Lying on my side on the bed at 3 a.m., I heard the ping of a text on my mobile phone. My heart felt as though it was banging against my rib cage as I picked it up, hoping against hope that it was Harry. I hadn't been able to bring myself to message him, but I knew one of the others wouldn't be able to resist telling him what had happened, and I didn't want to stop them. There was just an outside chance that he might still be able to forgive me, if they did. A one-in-a-million shot was better than nothing.

Message from Nan

Happy Christmas, love. It's already Christmas morning in Norway, so I know you won't get this until you wake up. I just wanted to say how happy we are about you staying on in New York and starting a wonderful new life. In fact, we've already put a deposit down on that world cruise I told you about, and it stops in New York in April, so we'll see you then! Billy and some of the regulars are forming a syndicate to buy the pub as a private club, so it's a new start for us all. And it's about time. All our love, Nan and Granddad xxxx

So the pub was going, and my grandparents were off around the world. Dottie had been right, they'd kept the place on because I'd needed somewhere to be, so my going home would only have put their plans on hold again. I was happy for them, I really was. But I didn't think I'd ever felt so alone, and a fresh crop of tears slid on to the pillow as I lay on my side.

I spotted the parcel Aunt Dottie had given me out of the corner of my eye and despite the fact that it didn't feel remotely like Christmas any more, just the chance to hold something in my hands that my grandmother had sent, proved too much to resist. There was a small parcel inside, but there was also a book, with a note from Nan.

I found this in the box of your mum's books I kept and I thought it might come in useful. Lots of love, Nan xx

I lifted the book up. It was a guide to New York and the cover had four different photographs on it. One of the Statue of Liberty, one of the Empire State Building, one of Grand Central Station, and the final one of Central Park. Mum had bought it long before I'd ever booked their trip, and she'd get it out every so often and tell me about all the places she was going to go to, when she finally got to visit. That book was on the coffee table in their sitting room for a least two years, but, as I peered it, another piece of the puzzle slotted in to place and I finally realised why I'd always felt so strongly that I knew Harry from somewhere. He was there, the dominant image in the foreground of the picture of Central Park. And when I opened the book and turned to the section on the park, he was in more of the photos. I must have seen his face hundreds of times. Mum had written on Post-it notes stuck to some of the pages too, with details about what she was going to order in a restaurant on Fifth Avenue, or the time of day she wanted to take a boat trip on the Hudson to see the skyline at sunset. And there was a Post-in note stuck to one of the pages with Harry's picture on:

I'm going to find this ranger, because he looks really kind, and ask him everything there is to know about the park!

Mum had discovered Harry long before I'd ever met him, and she'd been right. He was really kind, but he was so many more things too. It was almost as if Mum was trying to guide me to him all along, and if only I'd opened the parcel before I'd decided to leave, I might have understood that sooner. But now it was too late. I'd hurt Harry, and even if I explained to him why I'd done what I did, he'd never understand, because I barely understood it myself any more. I just wanted to close my eyes and wake up when Christmas was all over, but not even sleep was on my side now.

Flicking through the TV channels in a fruitless attempt to find something that might take my mind off the monumental cock-up I'd made of my so-called new life, I stopped at a channel that was showing a film that hit me like a punch in the chest. Gargamel was holed up in Belvedere Castle plotting against the Smurfs. It might have been dubbed in Spanish, but I lay staring at it for another hour, until at some point I must have finally slid into the oblivion of sleep. But even that couldn't last, and every time I turned over on to the bruises on my backside, it woke me up. Things really couldn't get any worse.

15

———

'Are you coming down, or do I have to send DeShawn up there with a sack and instructions to kidnap you, if he has to?' I'd finally answered my phone to Paula after the third missed call.

'I feel like death warmed up, and I've already told Dannie and Rob I won't make it to the deli today. I just can't do it.'

'Bullshit.'

I almost laughed. I'd heard of tough love, but I couldn't help thinking Paula must have gone a lot easier on her clients than this. 'I've been up all night, and I feel like I've been kicked in the buttocks by a whole herd of donkeys.'

'Yeah and I'm sitting out here in a wheelchair, freezing my ass off. So, are you seriously going to tell me that you're going to leave me out here, while you spend all day sobbing into your pillow?'

'Actually, that's exactly what I was planning to do.'

'How about we make another deal? You come down and take a walk with me, just a half hour out of your jam-packed day of misery, and then you can go back to it. I won't bother you again, and I'll tell the others not to try and persuade you to change your mind about coming out for Christmas lunch either. How does that sound?'

'You promise it's only half an hour?'

'I promise.'

'I'll be down in five minutes.'

'You better be, or I'll start telling people you've taken the battery out of my chair and left me here to freeze.'

* * *

'Okay, that was six minutes. You're lucky I'm so patient.' Paula laughed, and set off along the sidewalk before I had a chance to answer her.

'Where are we going?'

'Central Park.' She was going so fast, I was having to half-run to keep up with her wheelchair, and she knew it too. If I'd known how to take the battery out, I might even have done it at that point – anything to avoid having to go back into the park.

'Why there?' I asked.

'Call it immersion therapy. You might as well face your fears, and get them out of the way, or you'll never move on.' It sounded like the conversation I'd had with Nan, when she'd told me she was sending me to New York. I hadn't wanted to move on then, but I definitely wasn't ready to move on from Harry yet.

'What if I refuse?'

'Then I'll go and pick up the spare keys to the shop from Madison, and we'll all take it in turns to come in and make you talk about Harry. All day if we have to.'

'Is that technique in the American Psychology handbook?'

'No, it's one of my own.' Paula finally slowed down as we got to the edge of the park and I noticed flecks of blue paint on her chair.

I suppose it was an occupational hazard, in her line of business, but it made me think about that day at the art jam with Harry, when I'd thought he might be Parsy. He still might be for all I knew, but I didn't care. It didn't matter if he was a famous artist, an urban ranger, or if he got rejected from every publishing house in America. I loved him, simple as that. I just hadn't realised until it was too late.

'I don't know what you think this is going to achieve, other than the potential for pneumonia.' I felt like a sulky teenager, who'd been forced out on a boring family trip that they couldn't see the point of. So it was hardly surprising that I sounded like one.

'Just stop complaining and follow me.' Paula picked up the pace again, until we reached Greywacke Arch, where I'd seen the first Parsy. And then she stopped. 'There's something you need to see in there.' The pathway to the arch was cordoned off, but she led me through a gap in the barriers.

'Is it more street art?' My heart was thudding again. If Harry really was Parsy, maybe that meant he was back from Florida. I turned to face the arch, but I wasn't sure I could go under it. If he wasn't there, the disappointment was going to crush me.

'Paula.' I turned back to speak to her, but she was already heading in the other direction towards where DeShawn was standing, about thirty feet away. She waved her hand in the air, and the huge diamond on her ring finger caught the light. I suppose technically she'd kept her end of the deal. If I stayed in New York, she'd accept his proposal, and here I was. I might not have Harry, but I still had New York if I wanted it.

'Libby.'

I'd know that voice anywhere and I didn't want to turn around to face the arch again in case I'd imagined it, but I knew I had to.

'Harry, I'm so sorry, I...'

'It's okay, I know. Paula told me everything.' He held out his hand and I walked under the arch towards him, drawing level with a new piece of artwork in Parsy's now familiar style, opposite the one of the benches that he'd painted before.

'Did you do this?' I watched his face, looking for a flicker that would give his secret away. My heart felt as if it was beating ten times faster than normal, but it wasn't because I might be standing next to a world-famous artist. It was because I was standing next to Harry and there was every sign that he might be able to forgive me. Part of me was still scared to ask, so talking about the painting felt safer for now.

'Sadly I haven't got 1 per cent of Parsy's talent.'

'But you know who he is?' Rob and Dannie would never let me hear the end of it if they were right about DeShawn. The fact I'd be around to hear them say 'I told you so', made me smile.

'I know who *she* is.'

'She? Oh my God, it's Paula.' I didn't need him to answer, I already knew I was right, but he nodded anyway.

'It is. Sometimes she gets me in to help with parts of the wall she can't reach, but mostly she just adjusts her chair to do it all. But you can't breathe a word, she's really insistent about that. She thinks that using the wheelchair is what's helped her disguise that she's Parsy for so long. And she even times her tweets, so that they appear automatically, and no one will work out that's it her. Like she did at the Community Center.' Harry smiled, and I looked at the artwork on the wall behind him properly for the first time. It was unmistakeably my parents, standing in the Ladies Pavilion that overlooked one of the lakes in Central Park.

'And what about this one, did you help with this?'

'No. Paula took a photograph of the screensaver on your phone weeks ago, with the picture of your parents. I think she originally planned just to do you a painting, but the recent turn of events required something more dramatic. I was five hours in the direction of Florida when she called me, so she had to get DeShawn to help her with this one. We cordoned off the arch when I got here, in the early hours of this morning, so no one would find out that another Parsy had appeared, before we were ready.'

'It's beautiful and I can't believe she's done this for me, that you all have. You don't think the park authorities will cover it up, do you?' I wanted to touch it, but I was scared the paint might still be wet, and I couldn't bear for anything to spoil it. It was perfect, and my parents were finally in New York. Right there on the wall, in front of me. The kindness and friendship of the people I'd met here had been such an unexpected surprise, and no Christmas gift I could ever be given would even come close to how much all of that meant to me.

'Not when it's a Parsy; there'd be a riot if they even talked about covering it up.'

'Is she called that because she went to Parsons?'

'How did you know?'

'Because I thought it was you, that day you came to the art jam and your sleeves were covered in paint. I remembered you said you'd gone to Parsons, and I just put two and two together and made five.'

'She did that one without any help. I really was up most of the night, working on my submission for the agent.'

'Have you heard anything?'

'I got a call yesterday to tell me they want to represent me, and they'll start sending it out to publishers in the New Year. I was going to tell you when we went to the Empire State Building, when I thought it was turning into the perfect Christmas Eve.'

The boulder was back in my throat. I'd ruined his perfect day, when he'd worked so hard to give me mine and to make me feel at home in his city. 'That's fantastic news, Harry, but I'm so sorry...'

'You've got to stop saying that. I get it now, and I'm sorry that you were hurt, but in a weird kind of way, I'm glad about what happened to you last night, if that's what it took to make you realise that this is where you should be.'

'I'm glad too, but will you at least let me try and make it up to you?' I moved to kiss him, but he stepped back. And for a moment I wasn't sure if he'd forgiven me at all.

'There's one more thing I need to show you, first.' I held on to his hand as he led me through the park towards the row of benches where he'd found me crying that first day, reading Grace and Charlie's plaque. 'I might not be able to produce something as spectacular as Paula, but there was only one thing I wanted to get you for Christmas, and I hope I've got it right.' Walking another thirty feet or so past Grace and Charlie's bench, he let go of my hand, and turned me round to face another bench, with such a bright and unblemished plaque, that it could only have been there for a couple of days, at most. I read the words out loud.

To Mum and Dad ~ From Libby

You loved this island without ever seeing it, but you gave me the world, so I could see it all.

The inscription he'd chosen was so perfect and all I could do was nod, until I finally managed to speak. 'Those words... I don't know how you knew, but it's exactly what I would have chosen, because it's what I realised last night. They only ever wanted me to be what I wanted to be, and to go where I wanted to go.' It had been my father's wish for me every New Year's Day and they'd have been so happy I was here.

'I'm glad you like them, but you can change the plaque if you want to. I had to call in some serious favours to get it done in time for Christmas; it usually takes months.'

'But the website said it costs 10,000 dollars to get a plaque put up.' I couldn't believe this was happening, and the fact I had no idea how I was ever going to repay Harry had nothing to do with money.

'Ah, but I have the benefit of being able to pay it back through my wages over ten years if I want to. I just hope I find a publisher, or a roommate, or I might have to take up extreme couponing to get by.' He laughed. 'Seriously, it was worth every cent, and I'll hardly notice it going straight from my wages. It was never about the money, it was always about you.'

'And there I was about to offer to be your roommate.' I put my arms around his neck. I might finally have realised where the instant connection to Harry came from, but that still didn't explain why I'd fallen in love with him as quickly as I had, from that first day in the park. Perhaps Charlie had it right when he'd written the message on the bench for Grace – maybe some people could be in love before they even met. Or maybe the lack of sleep was just making me crazy. None of it mattered. I had Harry back, and I wasn't about to blow it again. 'No one's ever done anything like this for me before. You couldn't have got me anything better.'

'Wait until you see my final present!' Harry's dark brown eyes twinkled, and I knew he was up to something. He put his hand in his pocket and pulled it back out, with his fist tightly clenched.

'What is it?'

'Open it and see.' Peeling Harry's hand open, I laughed. There, in the middle of his palm, was a tacky plastic tree decoration in the shape of a Smurf. 'I thought we could hang it on our first Christmas tree.'

'Maybe around the back.' I laughed again, as he pulled me into his arms, and I already knew we'd fill our tree with decorations that meant something to the two of us, in the years to come. I'd always have my snow globe, and the perfect image of the tree I'd had growing up with Mum and Dad, that was so like the one captured inside it. Thanks to Paula, they had their place on the island at last. And, because of Harry, I had mine. It was finally time to make new Christmas memories, and I couldn't wait to start.

EPILOGUE

'I can't believe we made it.' I slumped down into the seat of the plane, breathing like I'd just finished a marathon. 'It feels like we've run all the way from Seventh Avenue.'

'I didn't want to tell you that I was ringing the airlines every morning to check for cancelled seats on flights before the thirtieth, in case nothing came of it.' Harry smiled and I would have kissed him, if I hadn't still been struggling to catch my breath. 'But I guess I didn't think it through, and I've never seen someone pack a bag as fast as you did.'

'All that packaging stuff up in the shop honed my skills.' I took hold of his hand, lacing my fingers through his and marvelling at the fact that I hadn't even met this man two months ago.

'Do you think your grandparents are going to like me?' He looked genuinely nervous, and I loved him even more because of how important it was to him to build a relationship with my family.

'They're going to adore you, and Granddad's going to love having someone to talk to about his garden. It's the only place he likes spending time more than at their pub.' I furrowed my brow. 'At least he did until they discovered how much fun taking a holiday can be.'

'Your grandmother has got big plans by the sounds of things. I hope we get to be that adventurous when we retire.' That was another thing about Harry that was so great; there was no second guessing with him where he saw this going and no playing games. After I'd split up with Ryan, my grandparents had admitted that they'd never been sure about him, and that my parents hadn't seemed keen either, but none of them had said anything because it had to be my choice. I knew if Mum and Dad could have chosen someone for me, it would have been Harry. And with the notes in Mum's guidebook, I still wasn't sure they hadn't had a hand in it.

'Oh, Nan has lot of travel plans. But they've already booked the flights to New York for next Christmas. Aunt Dottie is even forgoing her trip to the Bahamas, so that's going to be a proper family Christmas.'

'Am I invited?' Harry's eyes met mine and I nodded.

'Always, but only if we get to go and see your family for New Year.'

'You've always been with your Mum and Dad for New Year; I don't want you to feel like you've got to give that up for me.'

'I know, but this trip is about saying goodbye. Not to them, because I know now that they're wherever I am. It's just about saying goodbye to the old traditions, because I don't need any of those things to remember Mum and Dad. I can't thank you enough for giving me the chance to do this one last time, though.'

'It doesn't have to be the last time and, if you ever change your mind and feel you need to go back there, at New Year, or any other time, we'll make it happen. I'll be happy anywhere you are Lib, so you're stuck with me now.'

'I'm counting on it, because being stuck with you is the best thing that's ever happened to me.' Leaning towards Harry, I kissed him. And despite the fact that by some miracle we were en route to my hometown in time for New Year's Eve, it was Harry who felt most like home to me now.

ACKNOWLEDGMENTS

I want to start these acknowledgements by thanking the friends I met on a weekend away, when I was mulling over the idea for this story. We ended the evening of friendship and laughter chatting it through back at our hotel, and it was a great reminder that friends (old and new) can help make a brand-new place feel like home. Thank you so much Dannie Thomson-Maude, Rob Thomson-Maude, Karly Thomson, Abbie Eagleton and Paula Stroud for a wonderful weekend and for lending some of the characters your first names.

The book is also jointly dedicated to the friends, most of whom I've never met in real life, who make my online writing communities feel like home. There are so many lovely regular commenters on my posts, but I've used the power of algorithms to list the people they tell me interact the most, so thank you:

Mary Brock, Rosie Ward, Julie Hall, Suzanne Cowen, Edith Smith, Claire Griffin, Debbie Marie Sleigh, Gillian Walter-Browne, Melissa Khajehgeer, Claire Ellis, Kathryn Paddock, Helen Norris, Sharon McClintock, Karla Gilham, Jean Norris, Sharon McClintock, Karla Gilham, Jean Norris, Sally Starley, Michelle Hallowes, Jackie Bruce, Hayley Marsland, Lizzie Philpot, Emma Stokes, May Miller, Gillian Ives, Sylvia Nicholl, Sharon Gullet Norman, Carrie Cox, Jenny Vaughan, Valerie Findlay, Elspeth Pyper, Louise Farr, Lauren Hewitt, Anne Williams, Beverley Ann Hopper, Trish Ashe, Rosalind McKee, Honey Harrison, Wendy

Neels, Bex Hiley, Julie Foster, Sharon Booth, Ros Carling, Maureen Bell, Tanya Goodsell, Hannah Knox, Janet Wolstenholme, Lin West, Jane Bell, Isabella Tartaruga, Rachael Thomas, Audrey Galloway, Helen Phifer, Steve Dunn, Johanne Thompson, Joanne Aisthorpe, Deirdre Palmer, Jessica Redland, Grace Power, Meena Kumari, Suzi Harmer, Andrea Davis, Yvonne Delve, Katie Chapman, Sharon Bull, Rita Martin, Helen Rolfe, Kay Love, Tegan Martin, Debbie Blackman, Ian Wilfred, Mary Grand and Scott from @bookconvos.

I'm so sorry if you're a regular contributor and I've missed a name check, but please know I'm so grateful for all the interaction I am privileged to receive, with the best readers in the world. Thank you all so much xx

As always, I also want to say a huge thank you to all the wonderful reviewers and book bloggers who have done so much to get the word out about my books. I won't name check everyone this time around, as I did in my last book, because of all the names already listed above, but please know how thankful I am for all of your support and kindness.

Another debt of gratitude goes to my writing tribe – The Write Romantics. Thank you so much Helen, Jessica, Sharon, Alex, Helen, Deirdre, Jackie, Lynne and Rachel for all your support and friendship over the last ten years. What a journey we've all had!

The team at Boldwood Books are the reason I have so many lovely readers who regularly engage with me, having discovered my books since I was first published by Boldwood. The entire staff are wonderfully supportive and encouraging, but special thanks must go to my brilliant editor, Emily Ruston, as well as to the marketing team, including Claire, Nia, Jenna and Marcela. My wonderful and unendingly patient copy editor and proofreader, Candida Bradford, is someone to whom I am also incredibly grateful. A huge thank you must also go to Amanda Ridout for having the vision and creativity to set up such a dynamic publishing company.

Finally, as always, I have to thank my closest friends and family for always supporting and encouraging me. I love you all.

ABOUT THE AUTHOR

Jo Bartlett is the bestselling author of over nineteen women's fiction titles. She fits her writing in between her two day jobs as an educational consultant and university lecturer and lives with her family and three dogs on the Kent coast. Her first title for Boldwood is The Cornish Midwife – part of a twelve-book deal.

Sign up to Jo Bartlett's mailing list for news, competitions and updates on future books.

Follow Jo on social media here:

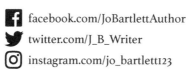

facebook.com/JoBartlettAuthor

twitter.com/J_B_Writer

instagram.com/jo_bartlett123

ALSO BY JO BARTLETT

Standalone

Boldwood

Boldwood Books is an award-winning fiction publishing company seeking out the best stories from around the world.

Find out more at www.boldwoodbooks.com

Join our reader community for brilliant books, competitions and offers!

Follow us
@BoldwoodBooks
@TheBoldBookClub

Sign up to our weekly
deals newsletter

https://bit.ly/BoldwoodBNewsletter

Made in the USA
Middletown, DE
03 October 2023

40112755R00116